WANTON

Lynn Michaels

Copyright © 2016 Lynn Michaels & Rubicon Fiction
All rights reserved.
ISBN: 1499694075
ISBN-13: 978-1499694079

DEDICATION

To my awesome Beta-reading team for being the best cheerleaders and encouraging me when I barely had the courage. And to the two RN Jenn's for help on the clinical challenges.

ACKNOWLEDGMENTS

A huge and warm thank you to
Jay Aheer and Simply Defined Art,
Devils in the Details Editing,
and Varian Krylov for the original photography.

Lynn Michaels

Contents

1 Punishment 6
2 Entreaty 28
3 Atonement 33
4 Possession 43
5 Concessions 48
6 Accord 53
7 Decisions 61
8 Endeavor 72
9 Exhibition 85
10 Contention 90
11 Reflections 97
12 Havoc 99
13 Fragments 103
14 Assay 107
15 Emanation 112
16 Anguish 119
17 Unraveled 130
18 Tumult 135
19 Redemption 144
20 Absorption 159
21 Recovery 168
22 Domination 177
23 Domestication 182

Lynn Michaels

WANTON

Down, wanton, down! Have you no shame

That at the whisper of Love's name,

Or Beauty's, presto! up you raise

Your Angry head and stand at gaze?

~Robert Graves

Lynn Michaels

1 Punishment

Corey stepped up to the bar, rapping his knuckles against the wood and ordered a shot of tequila. It felt oddly invigorating, and yet he knew it was a mistake. Eventually, Jack would come looking for him, and then? He shuddered at the thought with a mix of trepidation and delight, anticipating what Jack would do when he found him.

His sneakers squeaked on the grimy floor as he shifted his weight, sliding between the wooden stools. Jack would hate everything about this place, from the obvious filth to the low lighting, and especially the low character of most of the patrons. It was one of the seediest pick-up spots in town, but close enough to his apartment that it made a great place for hiding out.

He didn't want to need Jack and his games, but he couldn't imagine living without what Jack could do for him. Was that love? Having Jack in his life was difficult and potentially heartbreaking, but living without him would be worse. Was that a reason to keep going?

What was wrong with wanting a normal life, anyway? He laughed at himself because he didn't know what normal meant anymore. He only knew that Jack was his Dom, and he was letting the Dom and sub games get too...involved?

"What are you doing?" Jack's smoky baritone thrummed through Corey's body. Something akin to terror raced down his spine, but he held fast to his rebellion. He gripped the edge of the bar, digging his short nails into the wood.

"Corey?" Jack's voice, firm and commanding, made him tremble.

Corey turned around, reluctantly letting go of his iron grip on the mellow wood of the bar, fingers shaking. His anger slowly slipped away against his will. Seeing the confusion on Jack's face, he lowered his eyes, unable to stop himself from sliding into that familiar submissive role.

"Why are you here? I texted you hours ago. You know I don't like to be kept waiting, and I certainly do not like you drinking." Corey could hear Jack's sneer in every word.

Corey opened his mouth to answer, but couldn't make a single word come out. His heart seized up and his throat closed. Time stopped around him, narrowing his vision and thoughts to the man in front of him. Then his brain jerked forward, his thoughts raced and threw more unanswered questions against his mental walls.

Jack stood there with one hand on his hip. He jutted his chin up as he spoke. "This is a choice, Corey. It's always your choice. Is this what you want?" He gestured with one arm, to indicate the seedy bar. "Or, are you coming with me?"

Keeping his gaze on the floor, Corey let his black curls brush across his forehead and cover his eyes. Hiding still seemed like a good option, especially when he didn't really know what he wanted and Jack was always pushing, demanding.

"Do what you want," Jack said with a sigh.

Corey lifted his eyes and watched Jack, unable to do anything but stand there, as Jack turned around and walked out of the dingy joint. The heels of his dress shoes tapped a bitter rhythm on the floor. A slow ache built in Corey's chest, as if a hole had been ripped out. Jack didn't turn around. Didn't even glance back—just kept on going, as if Corey didn't matter.

He'd left without another word.

Jack's lack of concern had Corey coming undone; it was the one thing Corey couldn't handle.

Knowing that Jack hated this dirty, dark, place that smelled like sour sweat, had been the motivator, but Corey didn't really like it either. He just liked getting Jack all riled up when he had to come find him here. Corey had needed extra time to get his head together. But, suddenly the plan was backfiring. What was so wrong with making Jack work for it, anyway?

The door shut and Corey watched Jack's dark hair and thick shoulders through the smudged glass. A sob built in his throat, but he refused to let it escape. Normally, Jack would have grabbed him by the back of the neck and forced him out, dragging him home. That's what he;d been expecting. Shit! He'd really messed this up.

Corey took a quick breath and felt his heart pound a little faster. A part of him wanted to give it all up and just stay and drink Jose Cuervo all night—fuck Jack! At the same damned time, he felt compelled to follow his Dom, traveling down the depraved path where his sins led him. His leg started shaking with his mental paralysis. What the hell was he going to do?

He turned around and wiped at the sweat that broke out in beads across his forehead. He slammed his fist into the bar stool. With each hit he screamed, "Fuck! Fuck! Fuck!" His hair flew in his face, across his eyes in an angry mess.

Giving in, he tossed a ten dollar bill on the bar and stormed out, still unable to quite believe Jack simply left without him. He slammed out the door and followed after Jack, cursing the inevitability of it under his breath.

He shoved his hands in the pockets of his low-riding, baggy jeans. The chains he'd clipped on at his side jangled furiously with each step, banging against his hip and thigh. He knew he would be in trouble for dressing like this on top of everything else. Jack hated the chains and hated when he showed skin. Glancing down his body, Corey assessed his appearance and was willing to bet his belly button had been exposed beneath his too-short shirt when he'd turned to face Jack in the bar.

He was in so much trouble. Fuck! He really didn't like

dressing like a slut and hanging out in low-life bars. He just wanted to get a rise out of Jack, and didn't that just make him out to be a brat? No wonder Jack walked away.

He didn't catch up to Jack, but Corey knew he was headed home to his penthouse across town. Corey needed to get there fast. Jack had a car, but Corey relied on his feet and the walk would take too long. There would have been enough time, had he left the first time Jack texted him, but it was too late now.

He sucked at his bottom lip, contemplating just flagging down a cab, though he didn't want to spend the money. The alternatives were less appealing. Walking or waiting on a bus would take too damn long. The need to be with Jack, to take his punishment, pulsed through his body, riding the adrenaline like a wild horse.

This part of New Cabell wasn't fabulous. The newer part with the high rise offices and apartment buildings were closer to the bay. As a college student, Corey couldn't afford to live anywhere close to Jack, but he'd graduated and now he was newly unemployed and unsure of his next steps. Jack had been bossing him around for almost a year now, but being bossed around sexually was different than Jack telling him what to do with his entire life.

Corey looked down at the cracked sidewalk as he walked, moving forward and listening to the jarring notes of his chains and the slow roar of cars passing him. He'd get through this one decision at a time. The first was staying on the main drag long enough to hail a cab that would take him downtown.

It didn't take long before one stopped in answer to his outstretched arm. Riding in the back, he kept his hands in his lap, not wanting to touch the torn up vinyl seat.

The city blurred by him, small restaurants, fast food places, and strip malls turning into large hotels and office buildings. The cab finally stopped and let him out in front of Wolfe Towers, the huge apartment complex named after Jack. His company had built the place, and Jack owned the penthouse apartment at the very top. Hell, he probably owned the whole damn building.

Corey didn't know any of that when they first got together. He'd been working for a catering company that had been hired for some charity event Jack's company was hosting. Corey had been drawn to Jack that night like an alcoholic to an open bar. They'd been together ever since, and Corey didn't want to go back to his life before Jack. He'd only been existing before, surviving. Jack kept him focused and on track through the dynamics of their play. Jack made him feel. It felt real.

Groaning about his growing credit card debt, he pulled the plastic out and paid the cab. He'd been let out in front of Jack's building with its green glass windows. Corey sucked in a deep breath, wishing the view did more to calm his nerves. His calf muscles in his right leg spasmed in a shaky rhythm. Fuck! Get on with it!

He pushed through the front door and ignored the building and the people, if any were even there. He didn't want to acknowledge anyone; couldn't without a blush creeping over his checks. He fled to the elevator and jammed the button marked P at the top of the panel. In a few minutes, he stood in front of the sleek, black door to Jack's penthouse, searching his pockets for his keys.

He didn't recall leaving them behind, but it wasn't surprising. Doing a lot of stupid things to provoke Jack seemed to be the main course on tonight's menu. He hated himself for it, but couldn't make himself stop craving the attention he would get from it, either.

Taking a deep breath, Corey braced himself to knock and take his punishment for making Jack open the door for him. That was just icing on his masochistic cake. Terrified to knock on the door, but excited about it as well, Corey rapped his knuckles against the wood. He wanted Jack and what he had to offer so bad it nearly blinded him, yet at the same time, he wanted to walk away from it all. The indecision caught in his throat, choking him when he wanted nothing more than just to breathe.

Jack jerked the door open. For a moment, his eyes bore

into Corey with a fiery passion, then the look was gone. Jack frowned, his brows creasing above his nose. Corey trembled with dual amounts of apprehension and urgency that had his cock pulsing beneath the denim.

Jack stepped back and raked his eyes over Corey's body, top to bottom and back up again. "You look like you were trying to get picked up." His mouth curled up into a smirk, mocking him.

"Maybe." The word was barely audible on Corey's lips. He lowered his eyes and clasped his arms behind his back.

Waiting.

"It wasn't a question." Jack's tone was ice-cold.

Corey expected Jack to be angry, but not this freeze-out. Was he even going to let Corey in? Was he going to punish him or just send him home? Had he pushed Jack too far this time? Regret crept up his spine like little spiders skittering across a web.

He couldn't speak or move, as if Jack had frozen him in place to let his own yearnings crash down around him. He couldn't stop his eyes from searching out answers on Jack's unreadable feet.

Jack sighed and shifted his weight. "This isn't you, Corey."

"Maybe you don't know me all that well." The words spilled across his lips before his malfunctioning brain had time to reel it in.

"You know that I do. I know you better than anyone." His voice was hard and commanding. Corey almost sighed as he felt his body relax from head to toe with Jack's domination. He admitted he needed this, but did he want it? Was he ready to let Jack change the cadence of their bond? Was he kidding himself thinking he could possibly end this if he did want to?

Slowly, Corey peeked up at Jack's face. His features didn't give anything away, but his eyes were an inferno. His pupils were so large, Corey could barely see the dark blue rims circling them. "It's always a choice, Corey," he said softly, barely more than a whisper, letting his devotion ease out in contradiction to his words. Jack must still want him.

Corey dropped his eyes back down to Jack's bare feet, creamy white, long and lean just like the rest of Jack. He always had bare feet when they had their sessions. Maybe he would be forgiven and they could go back to the way things were before Jack's increasing demands on him, since he just couldn't move forward without answers and Jack didn't seem ready to supply them.

Jack backed into the central living area of the lavish suite. The huge white leather couch stretched out into the open space with complementary chairs across from it. Corey looked past him, purposefully studying the huge glass doors leading to the exterior balcony on the far side of the living room. The twinkling lights of downtown New Cabell showed through the gauzy white curtains.

He'd lived in this city most of his adult life after leaving his parent's house. His parents hadn't been cruel, they just didn't understand him and living independently of them had been liberating. He never once had a reason to look back, and for a while, he thought he'd been happy. Yet, all that time he never realized just how lonely he'd been, until he met Jack. Even with friends and classmates, none of them had ever been as intimate as they were.

"Come in and take off your clothes, Corey," Jack barked out.

Corey's gaze shifted, taking in Jack more directly. His arms were crossed over his chest and his weight was distributed evenly between his legs. Jack still wore his standard light blue dress shirt that he wore to work most days, but the tail was pulled out and hanging loose over his dark slacks and his tie was gone, leaving the buttons open at his throat. He was gorgeous and absolutely controlling. His hair was much lighter than Corey's and cut in a perfect professional style, while Corey's was shaggy and wild. Something about the contrast made him want to drop to his knees and worship everything that was Jack.

Jack's lips pursed together and his jaw clenched tight. It made his cheekbones appear even higher, if that was possible.

Jack was a living breathing Adonis; he was rich and uber-successful. His commercial real estate company had set records in sales over the past few years and his projects were award-winning. Corey was just some kid, barely out of college. How they had stayed together this long was still beyond him.

They'd been together almost a year, since the first semester of Corey's senior year at New Cabell University. Now he was trying to figure out how to fit this Dom/sub relationship into the real world, while still trying to figure out whether he really wanted it to continue. He didn't quite understand just what they were to each other anymore. Could they have more? How could it possibly work?

Jack stood there, waiting.

Corey swallowed hard. His heart beat wildly, banging out a new tempo in his chest. If he stepped over the threshold, he was going to be punished, and he needed it, as if the penance were some vital part of his body like his lungs or blood, but he was afraid. Jack wouldn't wait forever. Eventually, he was going to shut the door on him and go find someone else willing to play by his rules.

The thought that he might be replaced gave him courage. He took a tentative step forward and lowered his eyes, but not before he saw the smile creep up over Jack's lips.

The second step was easier. He shut the door behind him and locked it without being told. They'd played here enough for Corey to know the rules. The security in the penthouse was stellar; no one would bother them, even if he'd left it wide open, but locking the door was a declaration; a sign that he didn't quite understand but merely accepted. It meant the start of their session.

Corey slowly shuffled forward, unsure of his steps until he was just within arm's reach of Jack in the center of the living room. He knew he was surrounded by expensive furniture and he stood on an expensive rug. He had an even better view of New Cabell over Jack's shoulder, and knew it was an expensive view. All of Jack's opulence, his show of wealth, made Corey lower his head a little, as he stood there with his tight little t-shirt and slutty pants, smelling like cigarettes and cheap alcohol.

Did Jack think he was shoddy? Unworthy? His heart lurched at the thought. He wanted to be worthy of Jack and feared he never would be. Maybe that's why he was trying to aggravate Jack, so he'd push Corey away. So he would admit that Corey wasn't good enough.

He pulled his shirt over his head and rebelliously let it drop to the damned expensive carpet.

Jack scowled. "I don't like it when you dress that way." His words were severe, almost like an animalistic growl.

"Yes, sir," Corey answered by rote and kicked off his sneakers, dropped his jeans, and stepped out of them, leaving him wearing his socks and his briefs.

They were the red briefs. *Oh shit!*

He swallowed hard, remembering how he thought Jack would be pissed if he knew he was wearing the red ones when he'd dressed earlier that evening. Jack said they were slutty and wearing them out meant he was hoping to get lucky. Jack's possessive nature got him all riled up over things like that.

Jack scoffed. "As sexy as those little red panties are, I think you better take them off. Now."

Corey could hear the anger crackling through his voice. If he hadn't been quite so bad tonight, he would have smiled, ready for his atonement. He wiped the sweat from his palms off on his briefs, as he slid them down his legs.

"Socks too." *Bossy!* Just the way he loved it. Corey pulled them off and dropped them on top of the pile. He stood up straight, linking his hands behind his back and staring down at Jack's lovely feet with perfectly manicured toes.

His insistent Dom-voice barked his command, "Look at me, Corey."

He lifted his eyes, unable to deny Jack.

"You didn't come when I called you. I had to find you in that dive, dressed like this. Again." He pointed down to the pile of clothes. "You're supposed to be mine. You're supposed to do as I say. What's going on?" Corey had no idea how to respond to the gentleness that crept into Jack's voice.

Fuck if he had any answers! What could he say? How could he explain? Jack had always assured Corey that all of this was his choice, but Jack didn't understand. Corey couldn't walk away from it. Jack had him trapped, had wrapped barbed wire around his heart. He couldn't move, couldn't breathe. How could he move forward when Jack was asking him for answers and all he had were questions? Wasn't Jack supposed to have the answers? How could he move forward if this wasn't love and how the hell did he know if it was or not? Most of the time, it felt more like an addiction than love. He hated Jack as much as he wanted him. Maybe it wasn't really Jack he wanted—only what Jack gave him.

He squirmed and bit at the inside of his mouth. His whole world was collapsing around him.

"Corey. You have to talk to me. Tell me what you're thinking and feeling." He sounded desperate, pleading. Corey needed Jack to have the answers, already. *Fuck this!*

Jack asked, almost tenderly, "Corey, is this about you moving in?"

He exhaled deeply and nodded. "That's exactly what all this crap is about. Damn, Jack!" He balled his hands into fists. "I don't know what to do." He squinted his eyes shut, as if not looking at Jack could change anything, or stop the tears if they wanted to come. His throat burned like they might.

Silence hung between them for one long uncertain moment.

"I don't want to talk about it," Corey finally said, because if Jack couldn't give him the answers he needed about their relationship, then he couldn't move forward. The barbed wire scraped across his heart.

"Okay. Fine." His anger was back, along with his decisiveness. "But, if you don't want to talk about it, then you either have to take your punishment or leave."

"I'm here," he said, even though he knew his sarcasm would only make things worse. But, what else could he do? Corey shifted his weight from foot to foot, impatiently. He didn't trust Jack or himself. Yet, he was completely unable to stop any of it. He clenched and unclenched his fists. "Get on with it, already."

"Okay, Corey. I'm going to punish you." He sighed a little sadly and added, "But then we're going to talk about this anyway. Understand?" He spoke a little softer, as if he didn't want to talk about it either, but was resigned to the fact.

Corey knew it was inevitable and nodded curtly. He was too nervous to speak, but he let himself look at Jack, deeply, as if trying to penetrate his sleek exterior to search for what hid beneath.

Jack stepped closer, kicking Corey's clothes out of the way. He leaned in and softly brushed Corey's lips with his own before sliding his tongue across them, demanding to be allowed entry. Corey opened his mouth and let Jack's tongue plunge in. With Corey's involuntary moan, Jack pulled back.

"Go in the bedroom and sit on the bed," he ordered.

Corey scrambled to obey. He rushed down the hall, his bare feet padding on the cool ceramic tile in the hallway. In the bedroom, his toes dug into plush carpet as he sat on the edge of the king-sized bed, settling his hands on his thighs. The comforter was dark gold and brown swirling together, adding warmth to the room.

He tried to clear his mind and just wait patiently, but he couldn't stop himself from squirming around. Jack would make everything better; he had to. Jack was in the living room thinking about his reprimand. Corey was pretty damned sure it would be the worst one ever.

He couldn't stop wiggling in anticipation and hated himself a little for wanting it so desperately. His life had led up to the culmination of this: one messed up kid that didn't want to be a kinky, masochistic submissive, yet that was exactly what he was. He hated it and he loved it, needed it and craved it. That barbed wire slowly squeezed down on his heart, cutting and bleeding him.

Where the hell was Jack?

Corey bit down on his lower lip. The waiting would surely

kill him. He gripped his thighs tightly, trying to gain control and stop his head from spinning with crazy thoughts. The room was quiet, utterly silent. He would be able to hear Jack's feet on the tiles when he came to the bedroom, so he listened for those crisp steps.

His eyes roamed the masculine room. He'd been here so many times that it felt more like home than the crappy apartment he shared with his roommate, Dirk. Though he was straight and a little on the vanilla side, his roommate was generally a cool guy. At least he never gave Corey shit about being gay. Certainly Dirk was happy that Corey was gone a lot and paid the rent on time. Maybe that was all that mattered to him.

What was taking so long? Corey needed to get out of his head to that calm place where everything would be okay again. He bounced his knee up and down, impatiently.

He started thinking about getting up and going to find Jack, when he finally heard bare feet slapping on tile. Corey gasped. His cock jerked. "Traitor," he whispered down at his member with a mind of its own.

The sound of the door shutting made Corey's head snap up. "Eyes," Jack said in his best Dom voice, immediately forcing Corey to lower his eyes to the floor in front of him with just that one word.

He listened to Jack opening the large armoire cabinet with double doors, where Jack kept all his toys, across from the bed. Corey held his breath, wondering what Jack would pull out and use on him.

"Hands and knees, Corey," he called out while still flipping through various options.

Corey crawled up on the bed assuming the position Jack commanded him into. His fingers curled into the thick comforter, just thinking about getting spanked. A heavy paddling would surely be followed by heavy fucking. A tremble shook down his spine and sent his stomach on a tilt-a-whirl ride at the thought of Jack fucking him afterward.

A warm hand on his back side had him jumping. It wasn't

a smack, just a touch, yet it was enough to make his heart stutter. Jack's hand slid over Corey's rump, and then a finger tickled down his crack. Cool lube followed the path, and Corey let out another gasp as Jack inserted a finger into his hole.

"You seem to forget who this belongs to," he said abruptly, as if claiming Corey all over again.

"No, sir," Corey huffed with a pant of breath.

"No? Then why were you shopping your ass out in that dive? Hmm...? Answer me." He sounded all out pissed; truly frightening Corey for the first time.

In stark contrast to his aggressiveness, Jack's finger plunged smoothly in and out of his ass, feeling oh, so good.

"Waiting for you," Corey finally managed to wheeze between breaths. His heart and lungs were trying to out run each other and his eyes had already rolled back in his head.

Still sounding mad, Jack answered, "Oh, were you? Yet, you knew I was here waiting for you. I told you to come over."

"Please, Jack." Corey wasn't above begging, especially if it might take some of the sting out of Jack's anger.

Jack chuckled, resolutely. "I'm beginning to think you're a little slut. Are you a little slut, Corey?" He pushed his finger in and out, brushing against the inside lining.

Corey didn't know if he was teasing or serious, but the feeling had him moaning, more than a little, and he barely squeaked out his answer, "No, sir."

Jack's finger pulled out, leaving Corey to buck against nothing but air, wanting that finger back desperately. But Jack had moved into full Dom-mode. "Well, you better not be. You're mine. I do not share. Ever. Understand?"

"Yes, sir," Corey answered in quick response to the authority in Jack's voice.

A quick smack against his butt cheek sent pleasure rolling through his cock and into his stomach. "Please," he heard himself begging, but he wasn't even sure what he was begging for. "Please, more, uh, anything."

"No need to beg yet, Corey." At least Jack's words sounded a little calmer.

Something hard and unforgiving pushed against his hole, slowly sliding in. "Don't let this drop." Another demand. Corey had felt this before and knew it was a relatively small butt plug. It settled heavy inside him, feeling strangely comforting, like a mark of ownership or a gift from Jack.

"Stand up, here." Jack pointed down to the floor beside the bed. His words were full of icy commands, but the force had Corey rushing to obey and clinching his butt to make sure the plug didn't move too much as he stood in position.

"Hands out," he instructed.

Corey obeyed, splaying his palms out in front of him, offering them up along with his soul. He wondered if Jack knew the depth of his offering.

Jack took his wrists in his warm hands, then wrapped cuffs around them, strapping them on with leather buckles that made him feel safe as long as they rubbed against his skin. Jack clipped a short chain on the D-rings of each wrist, linking them together with a clink that made him jump.

Jack shoved him over to the one empty spot along the bedroom wall. Corey's cock twitched at the rough handling.

There was artwork covering most of Jack's bedroom. Some were cheap prints that amused him, but some were expensive canvas paintings, one-of-a-kinds from mostly modern artists, but none were too famous. He chose his art by what he liked, what spoke to him. Corey's favorite was the fiery portrait of a stoic young man by *Zhang*. Despite all the artwork, there was one section that was just bare wall. Jack pushed Corey against that open spot, pulling Corey's cuffed hands up just over his head and looping the chain over a hook that Corey hadn't noticed before. This was new and made his heart leap with excitement.

Jack tugged on his arms, trapping him against the wall with his face pressed against the cool drywall. The world closed in on him like a darkness, narrowing his view to the two inches directly in front of him. Corey breathed in short panting gulps, his heart pounding against the imagined barbed wire, threatening to burst right out of the sharp bindings.

The concern in Jack's voice cut through the panic. "Breathe deep. Corey, you have to breathe through this."

He willed his lungs to slow down and forced air in deeper. It was important to make Jack proud. When he was no longer hyperventilating, he felt Jack's hot breath on the back of his neck sending tingling sensations straight down to his cock like lightning.

"Corey. Even though this is punishment. And you deserve it," his voice was a smirk, but then he became serious. "You can still use your safe words. If you need to slow down or even stop. You remember your safe words?"

Fuck the safe words! "Yes."

"Say them now," he demanded.

"Red to stop, yellow to slow down." Corey had never used the safe words. Jack didn't understand that using the words would be like taking back what he'd already given.

With a softer, caring tone, Jack said, "Okay. I trust you to use them if you need to."

His voice was steady as he answered quickly, "Yes, sir."

"I mean it, Corey." Jack kicked his feet farther apart, and tugged them out so his face was pressed against the wall and his backside was out and up. His arms, wrist to elbow rested against the cool, smooth plaster surface. Thinking about getting spanked had his cock throbbing and leaking.

For a moment the silence engulfed Corey.

The crack of a whip cut through the false cocoon that Corey had imagined, and a second later the sting on his butt burned like fire. The wail escaping his mouth wouldn't stop Jack.

Snap, sting. Snap, sting. It continued, climbing up his back and scattering Corey's thoughts and feelings with every strike.

Corey cried out and begged. He heard himself whimpering, as he pushed his forehead against the wall. The single tail whip hurt. Stung. After a while, his back was a warm burn and he'd lost his sense of time. He could have been there for only moments or long hours. He only knew that this had to happen so Jack would forgive him for being so stupid.

The burn continued, his heart settled down to a more normal rhythm. Jack would set everything right. Corey breathed long and slow until it no longer hurt, he felt nothing but warmth, until his cries quieted and he was floating.

"Damn it," Jack's voice cut through the haze and Corey twitched, coming back to his senses.

His heart jumped and anger scrunched his brow up tight. "Agh..." he moaned, his body starting to feel swollen and achy. He wished Jack would keep beating him; he didn't want to come back.

Corey lay on his stomach on cool white sheets of the bed, unable to remember how he got there, until he felt the sting in his back and the burn in his shoulders. He couldn't shake the stiffness out of his arms. Jack softly rubbed something cool onto his back.

The punishment rushed back into his head and he choked back a scream. Jack cooed soothingly in his ear, "Shh. It's okay, baby. It's over."

Corey stuffed the thoughts and feelings down and closed his eyes, wanting nothing more than to sleep and forget.

"Corey. Wake up, baby." Jack's voice was soft and coaxing.

He opened his eyes and looked around, slowly adjusting to the low lighting. Jack sat on the floor by the bed with a tray of food in front of him. He'd changed into his black leather shorts and nothing else. The site of his bare chest had Corey's nerves tingling again.

"Can you sit up, baby?"

Corey pushed his torso up, testing out back muscles that felt like they'd been sliced through. He ground his teeth against the pain and nodded, swinging his legs over the edge of the bed. Jack stretched up and pressed his lips gently against Corey's. Testing. Corey reluctantly kissed back. Tears pooled in the corners of his eyes, but he didn't want to cry anymore.

"Here, I brought you some food." He lifted a piece of toast with blackberry jam up to Corey's lips. Corey opened his mouth letting Jack feed him for a few minutes. After the toast, Jack fed him artichoke pieces with a thick, cheesy sauce, then homemade chips with gorgonzola cheese and balsamic vinegar, one of his favorites. The flavors were decadent, and he licked at Jack's finger with each bite, enjoying the soft expression on Jack's face as much as the food. He kept his hands in his lap and let Jack take care of him. Jack tilted a bottle of water up for him to drink out of between bites.

Jack smiled as if this moment were the happiest of his life, and it scared the shit out of Corey. That look of bliss on Jack's face was far worse than the anger and the whip. His fingers danced along Corey's calf, as if he needed to touch Corey to keep the connection between them.

"Jack? Is this how it's going to be?" he asked, sucking up his cowardice.

Jack dropped the next bite back on the tray and frowned. "Yes. No. This is because—"

"You whipped me." Not a question, just a fact. He looked into Jack's face again. He thought he would see tenderness or guilt, but Jack was angry with his brows pulled down over his deep blue eyes and lines defining his chin where his lips were turned down.

"I got carried away. I drew blood. And you didn't use your safe words. Trust has to work both ways. You didn't say red, damn it to hell, Corey." His tone grew higher with each word.

Corey grabbed the bottle of water off the tray and drank it down. He held it in his lap and stared down at it as if the bottle could answer any of his questions. "I don't think I can." His chest tightened as he admitted his failure.

Jack was clearly confused as he asked, "What? Trust me?"

"Use the safe words. And do this. I don't want you micromanaging my whole life." He slung the bottle out, gesturing to the world.

Jack sat back on his heels and wrapped his arms around his long, bare legs. He looked uncertain. Corey let the silence settle around him, but it wasn't comforting. He missed Jack's touch, the lack left him cold and alone.

"It won't be like that. I'm not asking you for a 24/7 thing. I mean, outside of this. Our sessions. I expect you to be self-sufficient, productive. You know, a regular relationship, or whatever. Damn, Corey, what do you think of me?" He put his head against his knees. He wouldn't look up at Corey. It was disconcerting and more than a little annoying.

"I think you're a controlling bastard," he spat his words out like weapons.

Jack chuckled and finally lifted his head. "Yeah, but—"

"Doesn't matter" He had interrupted Jack for the second time, and was beginning to wonder at his own audacity, but Jack was smiling again. What the hell did that mean?

"We can work this out, Corey. We can establish rules, so you'll know."

Corey leaned back on the bed and groaned. His back was truly torn up. He leaned over on his side just to relieve the pain. The shock of it had his cock back to full attention, making Corey realize that even though he'd been punished, neither of them had had a sexual release. This session wasn't over. The realization had his whole body going stiff.

Jack moved the tray to his dresser and walked back over to the bed. "You'll always have a choice in this, Corey. The trust goes both ways." Corey was starting to hate the soft, concerned voice. He needed the self-assured, controlling Dom, yet he also needed a boyfriend to love him and he wasn't entirely sure how to get both things out of one man. He was tired of being confused and conflicted. Hell, he was just damned tired!

Corey looked up at Jack standing over him. His shorts resembled the shorter type of MMA gear, but were made of leather and had red trim along the waistband and the bottom of the legs. They slid over his ass like a caress. Jack's abs rippled above them, waiting to be kissed and touched. Corey swallowed hard, wanting more cold water to quench the hot desire running through him.

"You didn't use your safe words and neither of us had any pleasure because of it, Corey." Jack was back into Dom-mode with his punching words.

"Yes, sir."

"Get up on your hands and knees."

After a whipping like that, he didn't think he would be getting more spankings. He moved gingerly, but not too slowly, hoping Jack would give him at least that much of a break. As he shifted on the bed, the butt plug made itself known. How had he forgotten it? It slid around in his ass deliciously, as he got up on his knees. His cock pulsed thick and hard at the sensation, leaving Corey gasping and swallowing down his moan.

Jack got on the bed behind him and wiggled the end of the plug. Corey dropped his arms down in front of him, pushing his face against his own skin and moaned into his forearms. Jack slowly pulled on the plug. Corey groaned as it slid out, the inner ring of muscles tugging at it, as if they didn't want it to go. Corey didn't blame them, feeling empty when the toy was finally out.

Jack leaned over and reached around Corey's hips, slowly stroking his penis, making Corey groan even louder. "You've been so bad, Corey," Jack whispered as he moved away, yanking his hand and letting Corey's cock bounce up and down beneath him, almost painfully. Just a moment later, Jack was back with his fingers and hands rubbing all over Corey, smoothing over his ass and along his sides, careful to avoid the tender spots.

Corey hummed. "More..." He was lost in the pleasure and

warmth of Jack's hands.

"Oh, no!" Jack bluntly instructed, "Your punishment is not over and you do not come until I tell you to."

A plastic ring rolled along his cock, shoved down to the base. Jack was serious and more than willing to stretch out Corey's torture. Cock rings were no joke; Jack rarely used one with him.

Desire and worry played against each other again, sending his emotions into some kind of overdrive, threatening to tear his heart apart. He called out with animalistic noises that ripped from his throat, involuntarily. He couldn't hold back, couldn't keep himself together.

"Knees, Corey," Jack said sharply, bringing Corey back. He'd slid down on the sheets, but with Jack's command, he lifted up again, pushing his ass in the air.

Jack slid a slick finger around his hole again, slowly pushing in. He curled his finger, hitting Corey's prostate and making him moan again. "Ah, more, more."

He heard Jack's familiar chuckle, and felt a second finger push in, stretching him out and making him pant. Corey needed it! Wanted it! No matter what conflicts he had when he was away from Jack, in the moment he was wanton and depraved. "Please, please, please, Jack," he begged.

"Do you want this, Corey? Hmm?" Jack rubbed himself against Corey's backside, teasing. He could feel the supple leather of Jack's shorts sliding against his bare skin in a rough caress.

"Yes, please, please." There was nothing left in his head but raw need.

Jack pulled his fingers out, and Corey could hear him moving, pulling his shorts off. Could hear the snick of the lube bottle, as Jack used more of it. In another moment, the tip of Jack's dick was kissing Corey's hole.

"Jack, God, please. Please."

"I love hearing you beg for it, Corey." Jack's voice was almost a purr, as he started pushing in.

Corey relaxed his muscles and pushed back into Jack,

wanting to take him in. He could feel the cock head breaching his muscles just before Jack rolled his hips, sliding in. Everything was lubricated enough, and with just a second of getting used to the feel, Jack started pumping for real. Corey groaned at the pleasure as Jack's cock thumped across his prostate. The magic spot that felt like heaven. *Fuck*! He just wanted to come.

Corey writhed against Jack's onslaught. He begged with, "Please, please!" and he whimpered, "Jack, please..." His words turned into unintelligible sounds, moans, panting, and strange gurgling noises that escaped from his throat. His ass felt like the equivalent of a high pitched note sounding and ringing like a chime in his ears. It burned and sunk into the core of his being, molding him into something different and maybe better.

Jack came with a grunt and low hum. Corey felt his release inside him. Jack started to slouch over Corey's back, but then pulled up quick, and pulled his cock out even quicker. "Damn, Corey!"

Corey moaned and let himself fall to the bed, feeling the crisp linens rubbing against his hypersensitive skin. His cock still begged for release and his balls pressing against the plastic ring felt like they had swollen into giant balloons.

Jack came up behind him and pinned his arms behind his back, securing them with the cuffs on his wrists again, complete with the chain connecting them together. His heart slid into a safer place away from the barbed wire cage, a place made of leather and warmth. His dick was huge and hard, grinding into the sheets of the bed where he couldn't touch it, though it begged for more friction. Jack's semen trickling down the inside of his thigh, tied him to the moment as effectively as Jack's restraints.

"You will not come. You will not pleasure yourself. You will not. Not until I say." He could see Jack out of the corner of his eye, pointing at Corey with every angry word thrust out of his mouth. Jack was back to being pissed off and not letting Corey climax was the worst possible torture. He would rather have the whipping any time.

"Please, Jack," he growled and admonished himself for the tears that spilled down his face. "I'm sorry. Please," he sobbed, but Jack ignored him, storming out of the room, slamming the door behind him.

Corey's heart felt empty and alone. Jack had left him there, bound and helpless with the hard-on of his life, uselessly humping into the sheets. His heart fell back into the metal cage where the barbed wire squeezed tighter.

2 Entreaty

Jack's stomach rolled with disgust. He wanted so much to be a different person, to be like all the other normal people in the world. Leaning back in the chair, he knuckled his forehead. Why was he so damned demented? A monster? Why did he keep dragging Corey into his darkness? Even though Corey seemed to willingly let Jack do whatever he wanted to do to him, it didn't mean Jack had to hurt him. He needed to stay in control for both their sakes.

Tonight had been too hard; he'd lost control. He rubbed at his chest, as if that could make the hollow pain go away. There was nothing in Jack's world worse than losing control.

Oh fuck, though! When he was fucking Corey and had stared down at the bright red stripes he'd put on Corey's back, it had been a complete turn-on, an overload of fucking sexy. Corey's entire back was as red as lipstick with lines where the lash bit into the skin. Several of those lines had welled up with blood.

Damn! He was a fucking monster for marking his boy up so terribly and worse for loving the red streaked evidence at the same time. Corey was just so beautifully amenable and that played so easily into Jack's dark, sadistic side. Nothing got Jack hotter than Corey's smooth hips, slightly plump ass, and lean back. His features were perfect.

It had been a tough session for both of them and no

denying it. Being Corey's Dom was just not easy, but Jack couldn't make excuses. He needed to find enough control for both of them.

Lord knew he'd put in a lot of extra hours practicing with that single tail so that he wouldn't accidentally cross that line. All of that well-earned self-control slipped right out of the cuffs, figuratively speaking.

Jack knew the whip could be dangerous. He should have known better than to pick it up when they were so emotionally charged. "I'm such a fucking failure," he growled to himself.

When Corey looked at him with those lost eyes, Jack thought his heart would shatter. His boy was counting on him and he'd let him down. Again.

He'd had to walk away from the scene or risk really losing it, and damned if that was also the wrong thing to do. He fucking knew better than to leave a sub alone, especially in the heightened state he knew Corey was in when Jack had stormed out of the bedroom. He'd never done that. He'd fucked up the whole night and worse, he had no idea how to fix it.

Jack sat on his balcony, having put his leather shorts back on, and he was damned happy it was summer time. The wind still put goose bumps on his skin and perked his nipples up. He sipped the brandy he'd poured to calm himself down and glared at the cityscape as if it had been the source of all his problems.

The majestic view of New Cabell and all the glistening lights that normally made him feel invincible wasn't helping at all tonight; he felt pretty fucking shitty. To think the night hadn't gone well wasn't just an understatement; it had completely fallen apart and it was all Jack's fault. He should have known they were headed down the wrong path when Corey didn't answer that first text he'd sent.

He was completely aware that Corey had issues with using his safe words, yet Jack had whipped him until he drew blood all the same. It didn't even matter how hard he got watching Corey writhe beneath his lash or all the noises he made, calling out with the sting and moaning erotically as he hit subspace,

Corey deserved better. Jack should never have let it go that far. Should never have taken it there in the first place and certainly never left him alone. Corey should be wrapped up safely in his arms, not writhing alone and bound on the bed.

Damn the boy! Why had he been determined to push every one of Jack's fucking buttons? Sure, Corey didn't know what he wanted to do and Jack had been demanding that he make a decision about moving in, but it would just be easier if he could order Corey to move in. It wouldn't work, though, because this was bigger than the Dom/sub thing they had going on. Yet, that was all Jack had to fall back on.

Why did he need Corey to move in anyway? He could have just collared him for the next step in their relationship. Corey would have loved that, been happy to just wear his collar and feel that type of ownership; wouldn't he? Did he even want a relationship with Jack? He had no idea how Corey felt about any of it. When had they stopped talking about all of this?

Jack growled at himself, knowing damned well that a collar wouldn't be enough. Living together meant he'd have full access to Corey and demanding, manipulative oversight of the boy's life. Was that what Jack needed? He ran a hand through his hair and pulled on the short strands. *Fuck!*

Was that the only way he would be able to have a relationship? Because, he sure as hell never could keep his shit together this long any other time he'd tried it.

Controlling bastard, that's what Corey had called him. It was the truth. *Damn it!*

He sipped the last of his brandy and set the empty glass on the little side table beside him and debated pouring another, but his hands were finally steady. He'd spent enough time with his dark mood. He needed to get his head together and fix this. Fuck wallowing in self-pity. If he wanted to be Corey's Dom, or anyone's Dom, he needed to have his shit together. He was Jack Wolfe and he *would* get his shit together.

Grumbling at himself for wanting too much, Jack pictured Corey laying naked in his bed with the whip marks seething across his back and his cock begging for release. His own cock twitched against the leather of his shorts, demanding he do something about this mess. With a long sigh, he got up and went into the bathroom, fished the antibacterial ointment out of the medicine cabinet and wet a wash cloth with warm water.

Corey's eyes were closed when Jack entered the room and leaned over to release the cuffs. Jack grinned a little at Corey's soft moans. He quietly ordered, "Hands over head, baby." Watching Corey obey without opening his eyes had Jack smiling even wider. He adored his gorgeous sub. All that golden skin marred by him. *Mine!*

Jack sucked back his possessiveness and cleaned Corey's back, then gently dabbed the ointment onto the welts on Corey's backside. The worst of the damage was at the small of his back. Taking care of his sub now tugged his mind back to the right place. Yes, he just needed to take care of Corey and everything else would fall in place.

When he was satisfied that Corey's marks were taken care of, he nudged his lover's hip. "Up on your knees, baby."

Corey pulled his knees back up under him, leaving his head smashed against the blankets. He grunted softly as he moved.

"Shh. You did good baby," he murmured, trying to sooth his lover, caressing his thigh. He reached under Corey's hips and took his cock in his hand, stroking the length from base to tip, then back again making Corey hump into his hand while making desperate little noises in his throat.

Jack's heart pounded at seeing Corey so needy. It was the one time that he knew for sure Corey was truly his to satisfy.

He fingered the cock ring he'd left there and pulled it off, fondling Corey's shaft again. A flash of guilt crossed his mind at how long he'd left Corey like this, especially after the earlier punishment. Had he demanded too much? It was becoming more difficult to find Corey's limits. Sometimes it felt like his boy didn't have any. If a sub didn't have a line to cross, how was his Dom supposed to figure out where to push and where to hold? The whole damn thing threatened to drown him.

He swallowed back his worries and rubbed his adept fingers along Corey's cock, lingering at the tip, rubbing across his slit and feeling the moistness leaking out.

Intently, he watched Corey's subtle reactions to his hand. His mouth was open and his eyes were squished up tight, when Corey groaned again, "Please." His voice was so soft, so pleading, Jack couldn't resist him any longer. The tightness in his chest eased up a little. Seeing the lust and passion on Corey's face made all the frustration worth it.

He leaned over breathing into Corey's ear. "I got you baby. Come for me." Jack stroked faster, but it only took that little bit and Corey was shooting out, covering Jack's hand, the bed sheets and Corey's own stomach. Making sure his lover's release was complete and relishing the whimpers that came from Corey's mouth, Jack pulled on Corey's cock until he was blissed out, lying still.

"Lean on your side. Hold still, baby." Jack helped Corey reposition himself on his side, then he went in the bathroom and wet a towel. He cleaned Corey up carefully, not wanting to aggravate the whip marks by jerking him around. Hadn't he caused the boy enough pain for one night?

"Thank you," Corey said softly, finally opening his eyes.

"Do you want some Tylenol or something?" he asked, cautiously.

"No." Corey's green eyes reflected like a cat's in the dim lighting of the room, and Jack was just as taken by him as he had been the first time they'd met. Corey was the most beautiful boy he'd ever seen. In the first thirty seconds after seeing Corey, Jack knew he had to have him.

He stroked his fingers through Corey's thick, shaggy hair for a moment, before crawling in bed and pulling Corey against him snugly. His own hard cock forgotten in the bliss of having satisfied Corey's needs, he finally let himself drift off to sleep, listening to Corey's quiet crooning beside him.

3 Atonement

Corey woke to the heavenly scent of bacon and a cold, empty bed. As he rolled over, his sore backside brought the night before rushing back. For a moment, he choked, unable to breathe, remembering the sting of the whip on his back. His fingers grabbed at the sheets.

That imagined barbed wire pulled even tighter around his heart, giving him second thoughts or maybe even third thoughts about everything. Not just Jack, but his entire life.

He sat up and looked around at the sunlight trickling in through the blinds on the big double window, framed by the luscious art. In the dull light, the room felt gray, and even the vibrant colors of the paintings and prints were dulled. Maybe his own mood had cast a pall over everything rather than the diffused lighting. Why couldn't he smile and be happy about this? He'd gotten what he wanted, what he'd begged for—Jack's attention and a large dose of pain.

Padding into Jack's bathroom, he took a piss and splashed water on his face. Jack would have breakfast for him and he'd better face it sooner rather than later. He rummaged through Jack's dresser and found a pair of silky black boxers to slip on, and he pulled them up over his hip bones, letting the waist band sit low enough not to irritate the wounds on his lower back. Satisfied, he made his way into the dining room, almost ready to take on whatever came next.

Jack sat at the table pouring orange juice into a squat glass. "Baby, I thought I heard you. Join me." He gestured to the chair beside him. "I love you wearing my boxers," he added in a sexy voice, deeper than normal.

"Hi," Corey croaked out, unable to bring himself to say anything else. He delicately took a seat, careful not to lean back. He noticed Jack's cringe. That was good. Fuck him! He should cringe.

"Coffee? Bacon? Eggs? Here's some juice." He sat the squat glass in front of Corey.

Corey took a deep breath, and reached for the coffee first. French toast and fresh fruit shared space on the table with the bacon and eggs. After a minute of sipping his coffee, Jack grabbed a plate and filled it with food before setting it in front of him. "Eat," he said.

Corey shot him a look, but didn't argue. He took a forkful of eggs and a bite of crisp bacon.

Jack watched him eat with a curious expression on his face. What the hell did he want? Eventually, Corey couldn't stand it anymore and broke the silence. "I'm sorry."

"No. No need. It's over."

"I'm just nervous about all of this." Corey popped another piece of bacon in his mouth and licked his lips.

"Hmm... That's pretty sexy, Corey."

Corey couldn't help smiling. Sexy was the last word he'd use to describe himself at the moment. He suspected Jack was humoring him, trying to make up for the whipping. He was inclined to let his lover off the hook, despite how bad he hurt. "I asked for it, Jack."

"That's beside the point," Jack muttered, and took another sip of coffee and peered at Corey over the mug.

They sat in silence, looking at each other. Corey had no idea what to expect next. That barbed wire cinched down on his heart. He thought about the time he spent last night alone, waiting for Jack to come in and finish him off.

The clock in the kitchen ticked off the seconds, as he stared into Jack's dark eyes. His voice cracked as he accused his

Dom, "You left me."

"I'm sorry." Jack's eyes lowered and his lip trembled, slightly. Neither of them were happy about how it had played out.

"God, Jack. That was worse, ugh! The worst. Leaving me like that. I trusted you."

"Fuck! Trust? How can I trust you?" His words came rolling out, angrily across the table. Yep, Jack was pissed again.

"I'm sorry. I—"

"Damn it! Stop." Jack ran his fingers through his hair, thoroughly messing it up. Out of control. So unlike Jack.

"I know. It's my fault. I'm trying." Corey wanted to say so much more. He wanted to scream and yell and demand. He couldn't get his heart and mind around it, so he took another sip of coffee and shoveled a forkful of egg in his mouth without tasting it.

Finally, Jack cleared his throat and said, "I'm lending you my driver to go get your stuff today. Okay?" His question sounded more like a demand to Corey, and he started to protest, but his back stung and his shoulders ached. What the hell was he really fighting for?

"Fine," Corey finally relented with a huff. He felt his face flush red as he realized that he had given in, not only to using Jack's driver, but for moving his stuff, for moving in. "Fine," he repeated, as if to reassure himself.

Jack's smile cracked wide across his face, showing teeth and everything. Why not? He finally won. Corey was moving in. *Fuck*! He had no idea what would happen with all of this, but now, after last night's session, Corey was resigned to it. He needed Jack to be in control, to make him feel safe, to love him. But this all felt insubstantial. It felt like a power trip, not love. He didn't know if he could live with that, if it'd be enough.

After a quick shower, Corey put his jeans back on, but to please his jealous lover, he wore one of Jack's button up shirts that came down well below his waistband and covered everything. "Thank you," Jack said, helping him button.

"You're going to have to let me dress myself."

"I know, but not today." Jack leaned in and gave him a soft kiss on the lips. "Please don't take too long. I miss you already. I want you here when I'm done at work." Jack's Dom-mode was back in full force.

Corey kissed him back and muttered his own promises to hurry, and headed to the door. He was convinced that if Jack didn't really have to make an appearance at his office, he would be coming along to help Corey pack, or more likely bringing a couple of hired hands to direct. If he didn't get over to his apartment and back fast enough, he'd have to deal with Wrath-of-Jack all over again.

Before he left, Corey turned back. "I'm moving in, but we are going to have limits, Jack. Can we please talk about that tonight?" He had to figure out how to make everything balance. How could he give in to Jack's control, yet still be himself? He could easily lose himself in Jack and that thought terrified him. He barely knew himself as it was. His identity had become more and more wrapped up in Jack and what Jack wanted from him over the past year. He felt himself slipping into nothingness no matter how hard he tried to grasp that ledge.

"Of course, baby." Jack's words were agreeable, but his tone wasn't extremely convincing.

"'Kay," Corey answered, though he didn't really feel reassured. Stuffing his trembling hands in his pockets so Jack wouldn't see them, he sucked in his bottom lip and headed out to the elevators. He couldn't really expect Jack to understand when he didn't understand it himself.

The driver met him in the garage. Jack insisted they take his Range Rover so there would be enough room for his boxes. Corey tried to argue that he didn't have that much stuff, until he realized the alternative was the limo. There was no way he would willingly show up at his old place in a limo. It was bad enough that he would be handing Dirk a personal check from Jack for the two months' rent he owed for moving out early.

Dirk was a nice guy, but sometimes outspoken. He'd made his opinion of Jack known more than once. Mostly because he felt Jack was treating Corey poorly, and he cared about his friends. That made it hard to fault the man for it.

Corey couldn't worry about any of that. He'd handed control over to Jack, now he would just have to live with it. Wasn't it easier that way?

He strutted into his room and started packing, desperately trying not to think about moving, even as he mechanically went through the motions. The driver brought in a couple of empty boxes and jumped in to help with the packing. "You don't have to do this, you know," Corey said.

"Yeah, but what the hell else am I going to do? Sit around and watch you? Sit outside in the car?" He saluted the air with a raspberry and started dropping books into the bottom of a box.

The driver was older than Corey, but not by much. He had brown hair cut above his ears. He was almost as tall as Jack, but his body was thinner and he walked with a lanky stride. He wore a suit and tie, but the tie was pulled down loose, making him look more casual, more approachable. He'd rolled up his shirt sleeves and jumped right in to the packing.

"What's your name, anyway?" Corey asked.

He answered with a bored shrug, "McCauley, but folks just call me Mick."

Corey dumped a drawer full of underwear and socks on top of the books. "Cool, Mick. I'm Corey Roman." He stuck his hand out.

Mick shook it firmly and let go. "I may be new, but I know who you are." He was about the fourth or fifth driver Jack had hired since he'd known the man. He tended to go through them relatively quickly, being a demanding boss as well as a bossy Dom. "Have to say, you're a lot nicer than I thought you'd be," Mick added with a smirk.

Why wouldn't I be nice? "Well, who the hell've you been driving for?" Corey chided.

"You know? Just sometimes, uh, significant others are more demanding than the boss. You know?"

Corey gave him a tentative smile. He kind of liked Mick and hoped he'd stick around a while. "Come on, help me with this shit then."

Hours later, Corey looked around his room. Everything he owned had been reduced to three boxes of crap, a duffle bag, a backpack, and his laptop case. Anything left over was stuffed in the two hefty bags ready to be chucked into the dumpster. It should have been depressing, but he didn't like collecting a bunch of crap anyway, and was glad enough that it didn't take more than a few hours to get a handle on it.

Mick grunted as he grabbed one of the smaller boxes. "Let's get this stuff loaded."

Corey nodded and helped with the doors. Just a few trips later and all his belongings were loaded into his Dom's car. He stood on curb staring at it. Everything except him was ready to go. "Yo, Mick! Let's get a cold beer before we head out, huh? This was tiring work."

Mick looked at him and shuffled his foot. "I don't know, I'm still working, you know?"

Did he not want a drink or did he suspect Corey of delaying? "Okay, a soda for you. Come on." Corey shook his head and looked at his watch. Dirk would be home in a few minutes, and he wanted to at least take care of the rent face to face. He could delay that long. They went in and Corey handed Mick a soda and took a soda for himself.

Dirk came in a few minutes later, right on time. "What's going on Corey?" He crossed his arms and looked down his short, stubby nose, and pursed his lips together so hard they turned white. His short, dark hair curled around his ears and neck, making him look younger and softer.

"This is Mick. Jack's driver. I'm finally doing it. Moving out." He noticed that the sound of his voice was flat and uncaring. He stood up and dug in his back pocket for the check and handed it to Dirk.

Dirk stared at it for a minute. "Uh...can I talk to you for a sec?" Dirk gabbed Corey's arm and dragged him into Corey's empty room. He glanced around with an open mouth.

"What's up?"

Dirk refocused on Corey. "Listen. Are you sure about this?" He leaned in closer. His voice was louder than a whisper, but not by much.

"Yeah." Corey knew his answer was less than convincing.

"I can't talk you out of it?" He held the check between two fingers, as if he wanted to give it back, get rid of it. "What happens when he gets tired of this thing and kicks you to the curb?"

"Gosh, uh, that was really blunt." Corey pulled away from his friend and now ex-roommate. He ran his fingers through his shaggy hair, wishing Dirk would just put the damn check in his pocket.

"I don't mean to be, but I'm worried."

Corey curled up his nose. "I'm not a kid. I'm getting a job and I'll be saving my money. Then, if something happens, I'll be prepared. So don't sweat it."

Watching Dirk's face as he slowly came to a decision was like watching a clockwork doll tick through the different positions until it came to the end and was still. "I want you to keep the key. If you ever need a place to crash for whatever reason, that door will be open to you. Just come in. If I have a new roommate by then, you crash on the couch. Okay? You got that?"

Dirk didn't sound like he was offering a lighthearted "*someday—but I doubt you'll ever need it*" thing. He sounded like he was asking for a serious commitment. It was incongruous to his normal relationship with Dirk. They'd been roommates, yeah, buddies even, but Dirk had always been the carefree joker with his quick wit and charming, yet humble smile. Even while spewing his opinions everywhere, he'd kept things light. This Dirk was demanding something from him, yet Corey wasn't sure what or why. His sad eyes held a concerned warmth that Corey had never seen before. Maybe he just hadn't wanted to see it.

"Yeah. I can do that." Corey looked down at the carpet. It needed a good vacuum, but he wasn't going to stick around to do it. "Just let me know if you need another month's rent or something, and keep my part of the deposit, okay? For short notice."

"Guess it's not really short notice. You've been talking about it. I just didn't think you'd do it." He could tell Dirk wanted to say more, but he bit back whatever else was on his mind, and Corey didn't really want to hear it.

"I'm not signing up to be his play-toy. We have a real relationship." Corey sounded like he was trying to convince himself and frowned at that. No, he didn't feel fabulous about his relationship and he certainly wasn't secure. He still couldn't get his head around all of it, but if he didn't do this now, it would be over. He wasn't ready for over. Not yet.

"You'd know better than me, dude," Dirk scoffed.

Corey nodded, still over-examining the floor. "Okay."

"I'm serious though. Even if it's just to crash for a few hours to get away from things. You've got my cell, too. So, call me if you need a ride or anything at all."

"Jack's good at taking care of me." Another plaintive and useless comment.

"I'm sure he is."

Corey finally lifted his eyes. He wanted to see Dirk smiling and being happy for him, but that wasn't what he got. "You're not my mom. Don't look at me like that."

"Sorry dude. I'm sure it'll be great. Take advantage of those digs, right?" Dirk smiled wanly.

"Yeah. All right. I'm out of here. Later!" He leaned in and gave Dirk a man hug, complete with pounding of shoulders. That's how you hugged your straight guy friends. Right? Dirk was totally hetero, but he was also kind and one of the best friends he had ever had—still had. "I'll see you around, no sweat." Now he dreaded the move for a completely different reason. He was acting like everything would go on just like before, but nothing would ever be the same.

Corey crawled up into the passenger seat of the Range Rover and strapped in, trying not to cringe as his sore back pushed against the seat. He put his hands in his lap, lacing his fingers together. As Mick pulled away, Corey fought to be still and not look back.

A few minutes into the drive, he felt Mick's eyes on him. He would look at Corey for a minute, then back at the road, then look again. "What?" Corey had enough of his game before they hit the next stop light.

Mick's brows crinkled above his nose. "Can I ask you something?"

"Sure. What?"

"I would think you'd be like happy, excited, or something. You're moving in with your lover, right?"

"Yeah." Corey's voice was still registering that same monotonous tone.

"Damn," Mick said. "You don't even seem excited at all." He glanced at Corey again and then back to the road. "Shit, my kid brother is more excited about going to the freakin' dentist."

Corey sighed. "I am. I'm just tired, and I'll miss Dirk, my friend. You know?" He shrugged one shoulder, not believing his excuses any more than he thought Mick did.

"I guess."

Corey was glad the ride was short, so Mick had to let the conversation go. Under different circumstances, they might have been friends. They worked together well, Corey liked him enough, but he was Jack's driver, hired help. Knowing how Jack went through drivers, he'd be gone in a few weeks, anyway. No need to get attached. Corey didn't think they could be friends. A conversation about his complicated love life with someone he couldn't be friends with seemed inappropriate.

Corey's lungs finally relaxed, letting him breathe again when they pulled into the parking garage.

"Hey, I'll bring this stuff up for you," Mick said, as Corey started for the back of the truck.

"No, I can't ask that."

"I'll have some help in a minute or two. Seriously." Mick wasn't making a move to open the back, anyway, so Corey relented, taking his back pack and laptop case and leaving the rest for Mick to figure out. He wondered where the hell he was going to put everything.

He took the elevator up and felt his need to be near Jack grow with every floor ascended. He'd told Mick the truth about being tired, and his back was stinging, not to mention his stomach rumbling. Damn, he felt like a total mess! The last few days were confusing and emotional. He was sick to death of emotional!

He let himself in the penthouse with the key Jack had given him, still unsure of what to do with his stuff. "Jack?" he called out, but there was no answer. It was oppressively quiet.

4 Possession

Jack let himself in and dropped his keys on the little table against the wall of the foyer. The penthouse was quiet. He'd seen his driver, McCauley, in the garage before coming up, so he knew Corey's things had been moved into the guest room.

He pulled his tie loose as he patrolled his living room. He spotted a shoddy backpack settled on the floor by the sofa and Corey's laptop case had been dumped on the coffee table haphazardly. Jack had seen the laptop enough from the times Corey needed to finish school papers when Jack wanted him to stay over. At the time, Corey working on school at Jack's had been a concession, so that he would stay longer. Now the sight of the abandoned gear didn't feel right. It felt like that old temporary compromise and nothing permanent. Jack needed permanent.

His eyes flicked over the rest of the open spaces of the apartment. No other signs of Corey lingered anywhere. Jack's chest tightened as he walked down the hallway toward the master bedroom.

The first door was the guestroom. With a shove of the door, he peered in at boxes and bags of stuff sitting squarely in the center of the room. Not one had been opened, nothing unpacked. His throat burned with the need for a stiff drink. What had Corey been doing all afternoon? Worse, had he changed his mind about moving in? After all, Jack had pretty much demanded it, not leaving Corey any more room to back out. He prayed that decision wouldn't blow up in his face.

He shut the door and continued down the hallway, passing the guest bathroom to stop at the end of the hall where he could see the master bedroom door. Shut. Slowly, he pushed it open and held his breath.

Corey lay on the bed, clutching Jack's pillow to his chest and face. Asleep.

Jack exhaled slowly, taking in the sight. Corey looked much younger than his twenty-three years, lying there. He walked to the edge of the bed and scrutinized his sleeping lover. His black hair, darker than normal in the dim room, fell over the one closed eye and round cheek that Jack could see. His lips were slightly open, begging to be kissed. Jack felt his cock stirring at just the sight of the seraph in his bed.

He pulled his tie over his head and let his fingers dance over the buttons of his dress shirt without much thought. Captured by the site of a sleeping Corey, he was truly enthralled, and Corey wasn't even naked. Not undressed at all in fact, he was still wearing the button up shirt Jack had insisted he put on earlier. Jack liked how it was a little big on Corey. Hell, he just flat out liked Corey wearing his clothes; it felt possessive and greedy. He licked his lips and let his eyes wander over the rest of him. He was still wearing those horrid low slung pants and Jack vowed to have them burned now that Corey was living with him.

Corey shifted slightly, as if rejecting Jack's direction even in his sleep.

Jack knew he was a controlling bastard, just like Corey said. In his work, his anal obsessions served him well, but they had played hell in his personal life with relationships. It had become such a lonely detriment that he'd given himself over as a submissive to try and break the streak. That had been a—well—worse than a colossal failure, as they say. His Dom, Colin, had called him a fucked-up, dictatorial power-junkie. Lord knew the man had tried to beat the authoritarian tendencies out of him. It didn't work. At all. It did give him a new outlook on relationships and allowed him to step up confidently into the Dom role, and that had led him to Corey.

He pulled his shirt off his shoulders and unbuttoned his pants, letting his slacks slide to the floor. He crawled up into the bed with just his briefs on, and tugged at the pillow. Corey stirred briefly, offering Jack a flash of green eyes. Then, he pulled his lover close and Corey curled up against him and sniffed at his bare chest, humming quietly.

Jack ran his hands through Corey's thick, messy hair. Things were going to work out. He made a promise to himself to do his best to keep the Dom/sub role in the bedroom, if at all possible. He kissed the top of Corey's head, taking in the exotic-sweet scent of coconut shampoo and a slight undertone of sweat.

"You didn't unpack anything, baby." His first words were already breaking the promise he'd just made, but he couldn't help it. He irrationally needed Corey to be his in every way.

Corey muttered a soft, "Sorry." Then snuggled even closer, rubbing his cheek against Jack's pectoral muscle. His tongue snaked out, teasing Jack's nipple.

With a chuckle, the tension left him. "Were you tired baby?"

"Yes," Corey's voice was soft and alluring. He dared another tongue flick across the nipple.

Jack felt his heart shifting with emotion and clamped it down. He pushed Corey over onto his back, pleased that his lover offered no resistance. He peered down into Corey's eyes. They were like two greedy emeralds. Leaning in, he kissed Corey's lips, sliding in his tongue and claiming his mouth.

Corey kissed back, tangling their tongues together, until Jack broke off. He wanted to cuff Corey to the bed, but maybe his sub needed to feel on a more equal level. Moving in had been a huge step; one that Corey had fought every step of the way. "You okay?" he asked.

Corey nodded and chewed at his lower lip.

Jack worked down the buttons of his shirt that Corey was wearing. "How's your back?" he asked with concern.

"Okay."

He wasn't convinced. "Turn over." He pulled the shirt off as Corey flipped to his stomach. The marks were still ugly red slashes against that creamy skin. Jack dabbed on gobs of antibacterial from the tube he'd left on the nightstand, making sure the worst lines were well coated.

He tugged the offensive jeans off of Corey's butt and legs. He rubbed his bare thighs and butt, soothingly. Corey's little cooing noises played his heart like a virtuoso, shooting straight down to his pulsing cock. He pulled Corey up on his knees, and reached around his hips and felt Corey's cock that was just as thick and needy as his own.

Determined to make this more loving, he licked along the curve of Corey's ass and stroked at his cock, rubbing his balls, tugging gently. "I want you so much."

Corey breathed out hard. "Please," his sexy voice pleaded with desire.

"No begging tonight, baby." Jack would make sure he used plenty of lube and strokes that were long and slow, until Corey started keening for real.

His fingers found Corey's hole and worked him with lube, sliding and stretching and taking it slow, despite the low sounds rolling from Corey's throat. He added an extra finger, pushing them apart as he got Corey ready.

Then, he sat up, pulling Corey into his lap. Corey sank down hard on his dick, grinding and writhing with pleasure, working himself lower until he was fully seated. He wanted to watch Corey's face, but didn't want to push him on his back.

Jack thrust up hard, his need for Corey burning through him, and he jacked Corey off at the same time, hoping they would come together. Corey's thighs worked in sync with Jack's own. "Come for me, baby," Jack breathed and kissed the back of Corey's neck until they were both climaxing with grunts and groans and Corey's seed flowed over Jack's fingers.

After Jack cleaned them both off with a damp towel, Corey wrapped himself against Jack's side with his face pressed against Jack's chest. Jack threaded his fingers through Corey's hair.

"When we get up, I need you to start unpacking and get your crap out of the living room." He hated himself for not being able to just hold his lover and be happy in that moment. If he couldn't back off, he was going to lose Corey, and he damn well knew it. Resigned, he forced his eyes closed and thought about how warm Corey felt against his side and how right that felt. He'd said enough.

5 Concessions

Corey sat on his knees in front of the coffee table in Jack's living room. He might be living there, but he didn't own the place or anything in it. This was still very much Jack's living room, Jack's penthouse, and Corey would make no mistake about that. Everything in it was Jack's, including him.

They'd ordered Chinese food. He loved the Shrimp Lo Mein. Jack had steamed chicken and vegetables and had wanted Corey to get the same thing, but Corey didn't like the steamed stuff. He didn't like Jack being so pushy about everything, either. He knew what he was agreeing to before he gave in and moved, but it all still rubbed him the wrong way. Maybe he wasn't as ready as he thought.

After moving in the day before and spending most of the next unpacking all of his stuff in the fucking guest room, Corey wasn't eating damned steamed chicken. He was proud of himself for standing up to Jack as he sucked up his noodles and munched on another piece of shrimp, relishing every bite, even though it was such a small victory.

Jack stared over his glass of wine, watching Corey eat, making him feel self-conscious in his triumph. "What?" Corey asked.

Jack sat his glass down. "There's a gym on the third floor. I'll get you a passkey. I expect you to use it."

Corey could not stop himself from rolling his eyes. "I

thought you weren't going to do this."

Jack smiled seductively. Why did he look so good when he smiled like that? "I never said there weren't going to be rules. Some are negotiable and some aren't. If you're going to eat like that, you're using the gym." He pointed down at Corey's red and white box of yummy noodles.

"I don't always eat like this," Corey said with a snarky tone.

Jack returned the sarcasm. "I hope not."

Corey looked down at his food. Why did Jack smash every little thing that made him happy? "It's just one freakin' meal, Jack. Come on."

Jack sighed and picked up his glass. He leaned back into the couch. "The compromise is that I won't tell you what to eat as long as you work out. I want you to look good. If you don't keep in shape..." Corey hated how he left that sentence hanging in the air. How he hated knowing the other end of it, anyway. *If you don't do what I want, I'll replace you.*

Corey's eyes lowered. He sucked in his upper lip. He'd been here less than twenty-four hours and already felt the pressure. He squinted his eyes tight. He could not cry in front of Jack.

"Corey? I think that's fair. Why are you getting upset about me wanting you to look good and be healthy?"

"Are you serious?" Corey's voice was a whisper. He wasn't even sure Jack had heard him.

"What? You're making this difficult."

Corey shook his head. His fear had crossed over into anger, building up like a volcano ready to erupt. He couldn't keep his words from being sharp. "Okay. Sorry. So, the rules are what? I have to work out. Get a job, and jump every time you snap your fingers. Is that about it?"

"Fuck, Corey. I'm not saying that. I'm going to keep the Dom shit in the bedroom. Okay? And not every night. How many times do I have to say it?"

"You don't have to say it at all. You have to do it." He took the opportunity to shove more Lo Mein in his mouth before he said something he was really going to regret.

"Corey, give me a chance," he asked with genuine concern.

For a long moment they ate in silence. Corey knew he had to set the limits now or his life really would be a 24/7 Dom/sub relationship. He knew he wouldn't survive that with his heart and soul intact. It was just so damn hard to stand up for himself when Jack was just so...*much*, and Corey felt so expendable, like a crack whore. Jack could just keep feeding him pain, and Corey would jump through all of his hoops.

He'd eaten nearly half the box of noodles when he finally took a deep breath and asked the question that was really burning at him. He figured it was the best place to start. "If you're really going to stand by what you said, Jack, then why is all my stuff in the guest room?" He held back a sob. Damn, he was turning into a girly-girl.

"What? That's for you."

Corey just stared at his lover with narrowed eyes of confusion, mouth agape. What the hell was he talking about?

"Baby. I just wanted you to have a place of your own. A retreat for when things get to be too much. Plus, you need a desk where you can look for a job, and there's really not much room in the master for your clothes anyway. It isn't because I want to tell you what to do or shut you out. Understand?"

"No, not really." He didn't understand at all. If Jack really wanted to be partners and only dominate him for sex, he would have moved him into the master bedroom. With him.

Jack exhaled. "You will. Eventually. Right now just take it as a space issue and a place for you to work."

"Where do I sleep? Do I have to ask to be in your bed?" Corey knew his tone was creeping into sarcastic territory again, but it was pretty fucked-up that Jack had practically demanded he move in and then shoved him to the guestroom like he'd been someone to accommodate, not a lover, just the sub.

"My bed. Our bed. You sleep with me in our bed and no, you do not have to ask. I expect it. Come on, Corey."

He set the nearly empty box of Lo Mein on the coffee

table and stared down at the floor. He needed to finish this. "What about coming and going?"

"Corey, I'm not going to dictate that with you. But, I do expect communication. There will be events I need you to attend and when I need a session, I expect you to be reasonably available, just like before, that doesn't change. I want to know where you are so I won't worry. And Corey?" Jack went into Dom-mode, his voice hardening. Corey immediately looked up, hearing that tone. Jack's brows had crinkled down over his forehead.

"Yes?" His breath caught in his throat.

"I expect that you will not go to that dive bar or any place like it. You're my lover. You live with me. I expect you to conduct yourself better than that. Understand?"

Corey straightened up. "Yes, sir. I won't go there."

"Good. What else are you worried about, baby?" Jack swirled what was left of his wine around the bottom of his glass.

Corey took a deep breath. He had to get it all out and the hardest part was already over. He still didn't like the fact that all of his stuff was crammed into the guest room, but he'd live with that for now. He pulled his shoulders back, feeling the burn from the welts on his back as he shifted. It'd be a long damn time before he brought that kind of harshness on again. "I think we need a signal for when one of us wants or needs a session."

"Why?" Jack looked curious, not mad. That made it easier.

"I don't want to come home and find you in full Dom-mode when I haven't had time to adjust to it. I don't want to have to explain that I need a session in the middle of some cocktail party or whatever. I, uh, I don't think I can handle regular life just flipping to a session without some kind of warning. I can't have the lines blur. If we have some kind of signal, then we know where the other one is at. Makes it simple."

"You're pretty smart, Corey. I think that's a great idea. What do you suggest?"

Corey shrugged and looked at his hands resting in his lap. "Maybe a special word or catch phrase or something."

"Like...popsicle?"

"Cherry popsicle?" Corey laughed.

"I want your Cherry popsicle?" Jack wiggled his eyebrows up and down, humorously.

Corey relaxed, his shoulders slumping at the sound of Jack's laughter. It felt nice to be sitting here laughing together instead of dodging tension. "Maybe something a little less obvious."

When the laughter died down, Jack asked, "How about I feel like having ice cream?"

Corey nodded. "That sounds perfect."

Jack licked his lips, his tongue darting around the plump lower one. "Well then, Corey. I feel like having ice cream, right about now. How about you?" His voice had lowered, becoming sultry and Corey felt the stirrings in his gut and his loins.

"Yes," he said, lowering his eyes again.

"Go take off your clothes and sit on the bed, Corey." The commanding tone had Corey scrambling to obey.

6 Accord

Jack set his cell phone on the coffee table. Corey was in the guest room applying for jobs. Even though he was pleased that Corey seemed to be working hard on finding employment, he would like it more if he could just give his lover a job at Wolfe. Who was he kidding anyway? He wanted to give Corey everything. But as much as he wanted that, he knew Corey had to find his own way, his own things. He could only give his support and understanding. Corey wasn't about to let him get away with controlling every aspect of his life, like how he had demanded Corey move in. Jack didn't want to push his luck with it, either. His heart couldn't take Corey leaving him.

He hadn't really backed off the controlling nearly enough and he knew it. Since Corey had moved in just a few short weeks ago, Jack tried to reel in his domineering tendencies. Well, except in the bedroom. But, he still ended up telling Corey what to do more often than not.

Despite his failure, Corey seemed settled, happy almost, or at least content, especially after a good session, and there had been a lot of them lately. Jack couldn't contain his smile at the memories.

Corey had been right about having a code phrase. It helped stoke things up in the bedroom, heightening the tension and the level of play, but it hadn't helped much outside of the bedroom and they were still struggling with that. He lost his smile thinking about that outside relationship part, especially knowing how much of that was his own damned fault.

Jack was older, established. Corey was trying to find his way. It wasn't always easy being friends or even just being companionable. Jack knew he had been too tempted to throw them into a Dom/sub session whenever their time together became awkward. He'd done it too many times already. At least Corey had never rejected his desire to play. It would be far easier for Jack to just keep them in their Dom/sub roles all the time, but neither of them really wanted that. He just didn't know how to back off. Maybe they needed to take some time to get to know each other better outside the bedroom.

Jack found many things about Corey that he liked. He really had great self-discipline when he set his mind to something. Jack swallowed a lump in his throat thinking about how brave Corey was. He knew what it was like to submit and could never truly do it, but Corey's submission was total—complete.

Jack walked down the hallway to the closed door of the guestroom, not even thinking about what he was doing. He tapped on the door and opened it.

Corey looked up at him and offered a shy smile. "Hi, Jack."

"Hi yourself. We're going out to dinner."

"Is it dinnertime already?"

Jack lifted his wrist, looking at his watch. "You must really be concentrating. Yes, and I'm hungry. Go clean up and wear something nice. Slacks, polo. Maybe that dark green one." He caught himself telling Corey what to do again and added a tentative, "please?"

Corey rewarded him with a smile as he moved to comply, closing up his laptop.

Jack had bought Corey new clothes, nice clothes, including two good suites that he desperately needed. Unfortunately, Corey had fought and argued the entire time. Jack had eventually bent the boy over and smacked his ass in the dressing room. Jack had been amazed at how it calmed him down immediately. He'd wished he had a butt plug with him. That would really have kept Corey in line. The little spanking was enough over the line, though and Jack got his way. He needed Corey to have a better wardrobe. End of discussion.

"Okay," Corey muttered.

Jack stepped into the room and pulled the shirt he wanted Corey to wear out of the closet. Corey pulled on his slacks and stood in the middle of the room, obediently waiting as Jack tugged the polo over his head. He tugged it straight, examining Corey. "Yes, nice," Jack said. "I like this. Brush your hair."

He made his way to the master suite to clean up and wash his face. He wanted to take Corey somewhere nice. It would be an opportunity to share something more.

The restaurant was one of Jack's favorites. The decor was pristine and crisp, yet warm. The walls were all peaches and cream with vibrant art throughout and topiary plants in all the right places offering their green accents. The ceilings vaulted diagonally overhead, creating a great metallic archway. At one end of the giant dinning space, a fireplace burned a real fire, making the restaurant smell like oak and spice beneath the heavenly food wafting through the air, all tomatoes and garlic. The table linens were an immaculate white and the dishes were elegant china. The atmosphere was cozy, warm, romantic even, and Jack liked sharing it with Corey. A sweet hum of contentment rolled through his chest.

They were seated relatively quickly. Jack wasn't surprised, he'd been here many times and the staff was starting to recognize him from his frequency and generous tipping habits.

Corey's expressions were carefully checked, and Jack wondered if he was impressed or overwhelmed.

They were handed menus, but Jack ignored his to watch Corey's eyes scan up and down the long card, his lips pulling farther and farther into a frown. "Order whatever you want.

This is my treat."

"Are we celebrating?" Corey asked, his voice quivering slightly.

Jack wasn't sure how to read Corey in this new situation. He didn't like being unsure. "No. Things have been going well, though. I wanted to treat you."

Corey's eyes flicked back to the menu. Ah! Jack realized Corey was uncomfortable and feeling out of place.

He looked divine in the dark green polo that made his eyes look like precious emeralds. Jack couldn't stop watching his derriere when they'd walked in, as Corey's slacks were cut perfectly to show off his muscled legs. Corey had taken Jack's desire to heart, working out in the gym daily, and it was beginning to show. He looked great and should be confident. Jack wanted that for him.

He watched for a moment as Corey started squirming. "What is it, babe?"

Corey peered over the menu card. "I don't know what to order."

"Would you like me to do the honors?"

Corey nodded, and lowered his eyes. Jack's heart lurched. He loved seeing Corey so demure. He reveled in the fact that he would order everything, conduct the dinner, and Corey wouldn't fight or argue about any of it. He felt his body responding to his domineering ideas. He wished he could feed Corey from his fingers during this meal. The thought made his cock bulge. He coughed in his fist and examined the menu, trying to tamp down his excitement. "Thank you," he said, breathing deeply through his nose, trying to calm down.

"For what?" Corey asked.

"Letting me do this."

Corey put the menu on the table and rested his hands in his lap. "It makes you happy."

"Yes. I like it. I want you to be happy, too."

"I'm happy you asked first." The light caught in his eyes, making them sparkle. It took Jack's breath away.

"Are you happy? I mean with us, not dinner."

Corey nodded.

"I need you to say it." Like making Corey say the safe words before each session, although he never used them, Jack needed to hear it from Corey's lips directly.

He leaned forward with a sly smile. "I'm happy, Jack. So far, it's been better than I expected. Thank you."

His words sounded sincere. Jack would have to trust that. "Okay, baby."

He ordered oysters for an appetizer and sea bass for the main course. They had wine, suggested by the sommelier. A nice white with the oysters and a rose with the fish. Jack didn't want anything too dry or complex when Corey rarely drank wine. He ordered an Eiswein for desert rather than an actual dessert. It finished off their meal with a crisp finesse but didn't leave everything heavy in their stomachs. The meal was fabulous and Jack enjoyed the delighted little noises Corey made with every new taste.

"I love sharing this with you," he said. He enjoyed giving Corey new experiences and looked forward to more of the same with him going forward. Bringing Corey into his life as more than his sub was going to be fabulous and fulfilling. He couldn't help the smile that spread across his face from just thinking about it.

Corey smiled shyly. "I like it too, when you aren't shoving it all down my throat."

Jack reached across the table and took Corey's hand. "I don't mean to. I'm just used to having control. I'm trying."

His lip turned up on one side. "Well, I admit this is nice." He glanced around the restaurant.

"Let's go home and have ice cream then...hmm?"

Corey's expression changed. He leered at Jack. His tongue jutted out quickly across his lip, then back in, making Jack want to take his mouth right there in the middle of the restaurant.

Jack paid the bill quickly and a few moments later, they were in the back of the limo. "Come here." Jack couldn't wait any longer.

Corey obeyed, and Jack pulled him up against his chest.

He grabbed Corey's face by his chin and tilted it upward. "You don't know what you to do me, Corey." He assaulted Corey's mouth, his tongue shooting in and out of Corey's lips. "Damn, you are so hot," he whispered as he pulled back from the kiss. His hands had pulled Corey's shirt from his pants, as if they had a mind of their own, and they wanted to feel skin; they wanted Corey naked.

He shuffled Corey around until he was straddling Jack's waist, facing him. His hands traveled up the inside of Corey's shirt and found his nipples, pinching them both simultaneously. "I'm going to use clamps on these." His voice was breathy. He felt Corey's heartbeat speed up beneath his fingertips. "You like that?" he asked, huskily.

"Yes."

"Mm. Good." He leaned forward and licked at Corey's lips, pleased that Corey leaned into his touch. He pinched the nipples harder and watched Corey's eyes flutter. He bit down hard on Corey's bottom lip and Corey made a deep sound in the back of his throat. "Feel how hard you make me, baby."

Corey's fingers lightly flitted over Jack's crotch in response, making Jack want so much more, but he had to make himself wait until they got home.

He had refrained from using pain with Corey since he'd moved in, or rather since he'd whipped him. He knew how much his lover liked it, though. Jack liked it too, probably too much. Corey responded to pain like nothing else, and it turned him on to watch Corey's reactions. He wanted to give him pain with their session, but part of him was still afraid. He didn't trust himself to know when to stop and didn't trust Corey to stop him. Withholding him pain had been a different kind of sadistic act. Corey seemed to need it.

Corey's fingers became more incessant, and his cock throbbed against his hands through his pants. "Corey." He grabbed his wrists and twisted them behind his back. Their chests were pushed together, and Corey's face rested under his chin, his hot breath burning into his neck. "Baby. God, so hot. Corey. I want to hurt you tonight. Do you want that?"

"God, yes! Please, more."

"I want to, but...I don't know, baby."

"Jack, please. It's been too long." Corey's words tickled across Jack's breast bone in a hot demand.

He pulled up on Corey's arms, knowing he would be getting tight aches in his shoulders and upper arms, just enough to know he had Corey's attention. "Corey. We can't play like that if you won't use your safe words."

"Please, please, please." Corey was moaning into Jack's skin, his lips caressing Jack's neck in fluttery kisses. His hips pumped in grinding rhythm, seeking out more friction.

"I'm serious baby. Look at me." He released Corey's arms.

Slowly, Corey leaned back and let his gaze meet Jack's own. "I need it..." His voice was strangled as if Corey were holding back a sob.

Jack rubbed Corey's arms along his biceps. His muscles had already become so much more defined from his workouts. "I know, baby. You have to be able to say the words."

Corey's eyes filled with tears that threatened to drop. He started to say something, then shut his mouth hard.

"I mean it. If I can't trust you to say when to stop, use your safe words, we can't play."

"I'll try."

Jack pushed Corey over to the seat so they were sitting side by side. He debated whether it was worth it to continue the conversation. "I want to make you cry, Corey. Make no mistake. But, I want your tears because I've worked you over hard, not because you're too stubborn..." He let his words trail off. Corey damned well knew what he meant.

Corey sat back against the seat and laced his hands together in his lap.

Jack turned to stare out the window. "Corey. I'm trying. I know I'm controlling, but I'm not totally smothering you. Am I?"

"No, sir." Corey's voice was soft, submissive. Jack knew he'd slid into the role somewhere during their argument.

"Then, you have to do your part."

Corey breathed out hard. "I said I would try, sir."

"Look at me."

Corey turned his head and slowly lifted his eyes.

"Not s*ir*—no, this is you and me in a relationship. Not Dom to sub. Understand?"

Corey gave a nod, and Jack could tell he was fighting to keep eye-contact. "Yes, Jack." His knee started bouncing up and down quickly.

"If we play without safe words, then I need to know exactly what you want and how far you want it to go before we start playing. There will be no surprises. Can you do that?"

Corey didn't answer. His gaze started jumping around the car and he was wiggling in his seat. That leg practically vibrated with motion. Clearly, Jack had made him uncomfortable. Where was his line? Were they pushing it?

"It's one or the other, or we don't play with pain. It's up to you. Think about it."

The rest of the short trip home was quiet. Corey continued to fidget. Jack wanted to scoop him up and plant kisses all over his face and tell him everything would be all right, but he couldn't. He was determined that Corey start making some of these decisions. How could he satisfy all of his needs, if Corey couldn't verbalize what he needed and wanted, and, more importantly for them, when to stop. If he wanted to keep Corey, he had to put that first.

Jack crossed his arms, grasping his elbows tightly, determined to keep his longings under control.

7 Decisions

Corey's thoughts bounced around in his head as if his brain was a trampoline. Jack sat so close to him in the back of the limo, his body heat making it hard to focus on anything else. He wanted to move away and he wanted to move closer, to be sitting in Jack's lap again, so close he could feel him breathing. He wanted to feel Jack pinching his nipple and biting at his lips. The man drove him insane. The waiting would kill him. He needed to feel the pain. It was as if just by mentioning it, Jack had opened up his own little masochistic Pandora's Box of greedy desire.

They hadn't played with pain since Jack had punished him before he moved in, and those welts were long healed and grown cold on his back. When Jack offered the pain, Corey thought he was going to ejaculate in his pants right there in the limo. Seriously thinking about getting some pain-play in with Jack had his cock dancing in his pants. He needed it, and if it didn't happen soon, he would either act out to force Jack to punish him, or he'd end up inflicting it on himself like he used to do before he'd met Jack.

He hadn't even realized how close he was to that until Jack had stirred him up. They'd played around in their sessions, but Jack had been careful to keep it sensuous. He used restraints and toys, but nothing painful, nothing nearly intense enough.

He loathed himself for needing it so badly. He was

terrified that Jack wasn't going to follow through. He was demanding that Corey assert himself. If he wanted the pain, he had to choose between two things that he couldn't do.

He couldn't use the safe words. In the heat of the moment, Corey would never say stop. He needed the pain too much and it didn't matter how bad it was. The more pain, the more he floated.

How could he say what he wanted before they started? Part of the experience was not knowing what would come and not knowing how far it would go. "Jack?" he asked.

Jack turned to face him. His hair was getting a little long in the front, and his bangs slid across his forehead and over his dark blue eyes. "Yes?"

He took a deep breath. "I trust that you won't seriously hurt me. Isn't that enough?"

"No, baby. It's not." He turned again to look out the window.

They were pulling into the parking garage. Corey felt like he was out of time. If he didn't answer, he couldn't get his itch scratched. "I'm trying to tell you, Jack. It's so hard." He closed his eyes, squinting them together and grinding his teeth.

Jack pulled him up into a hug. It felt so much better against the heat of his body. "I know it's hard." Jack kissed Corey's head. "But, we have to talk about it. I can't stand—I won't—Damn, Corey. I need you to tell me what's going on in your head." He kissed him again, thumbing across Corey's temples.

"I need to feel the pain. It does something to me. When I'm there, I can't stop. I can't!"

"So, let's lay it out before hand."

Corey pulled away from Jack, though reluctantly. "I can't. I don't want to know what's coming." He folded his hands in his lap and turned to the window. How could he possibly describe this to Jack? He needed the control, the pain. He'd lied to Jack in the restaurant, sort of. He wasn't happy most of the time. He put up with Jack bossing him around, hoping for this moment when Jack would initiate the impact-play or something with a little more sting to it. He's been waiting for Jack to step up.

The car was parked and Mick got out, making his way around to Jack's side of the limo, and the door opened.

"We'll talk more upstairs. Come on, baby." He reached out his hand to Corey, so he took it as a good sign and grabbed Jack's hand. Jack pulled him out of the car and led him to the elevator. They held hands all the way up.

When they stepped inside the apartment, Jack let go. Corey walked in and stood in front of him in the foyer. "Jack?"

"Yes?"

"I don't think you could ever push me far enough that I would say red. Ever."

Jack looked uncertain. His eyes narrowed and his lips pursed together tightly. "That kind of scares me, baby."

Corey pulled his shirt off. "It scares me what will happen if you don't hurt me."

"What do you mean?"

"I don't know." Corey rubbed his face in his hands. He had no idea how to explain it. He needed the pain more than he needed Jack.

"Corey?" Jack sounded unsure, scared. Corey needed him to take control.

He sunk to his knees and reached out to touch Jack behind his thighs. He looked up Jack's svelte body. "I need this. Please?" He would beg for it. He needed it. He wanted to beg for it. "Please..."

"Okay. Go. Go get ready."

Corey dashed to the bedroom, stripping his pants along the way. He didn't even know where they landed. He sat naked on the bed with his hands on his thighs, trying to keep his leg from bouncing him off the bed. He hoped Jack wouldn't make him wait too long.

In a moment, Jack strode in, shirtless. Corey watched as he dropped his slacks to the floor and stepped out of them. He slid out of his briefs and grabbed his *Jammer* swim trunks, black with a red and white stripe up one side. They hugged the curves of his muscular thighs perfectly.

Jack stepped in front of Corey with his bare chest, bare feet, and snug shorts. Corey's hands and feet were tingling in anticipation and the need to touch Jack. "Breathe, Corey."

"Yes, Sir." He forced himself to take long deep breaths.

"I'm going to make you use your safe words a few times through this. Maybe you will learn how to use the words."

"Yes, Sir," Corey answered, but he knew it didn't matter.

Jack cuffed him and looped the chain over the hook on the wall where he'd been whipped before, but this time, his back was against the wall. He watched Jack dig around in the top drawer of his toy cabinet. Corey held his breath.

Jack came back and held up a set of nipple clamps. They looked like two shiny, silver cages strung together with a long silver chain. "Okay?" Jack asked.

"Yes, please." Corey was quick to respond. He felt his cock surge before Jack fastened the first clamp. If he hadn't been strung taut, he'd be wiggling around uncontrollably.

"Oh, look at yourself. Damn, that is so hot."

Corey looked down at the chain linking his nipples. The sight was something, but the pain in his nipples was what he focused on. It felt so good, hard and demanding. The heat in his nipples had him calming almost immediately.

"Is this okay, Corey?"

"Yes, sir."

Jack pulled on the chain. The pain in his nipples shot right to his cock, and Corey felt his eyes roll to the back of his head. "More," he groaned.

"Nope. I'm not doing anything else until you use your safe words."

Corey gulped at the air. He needed more. "What?" He couldn't think straight. He was already half way to floating. "No. More. I want..."

"Corey. At least give me a yellow. Then, we can keep going."

"Yellow, yellow, damn it. Go, more."

He opened his eyes and saw Jack shaking his head. This

wasn't going to work.

"Damn it, Jack. I want more. Yellow means to slow down. I don't want to slow down. I don't want to stop. Don't you understand?"

"Maybe not."

"Fuck!" Corey called out in his frustration and tapped his head back against the wall with a thump.

A whip crack sounded suddenly, and Corey felt it against his thigh, stinging and making him jump. It was the viper quirt that Jack had bought when they'd first started talking about pain-play, nearly six months ago. They'd never used it, but it stung nicely against his thigh. Corey looked down and saw a thin red welt appear. He smiled. His racing heart was starting to slow. "Better?" Jack asked.

Corey looked up at him. "Yes, sir."

"Good. I want to put a collar on you. Okay?"

"Yes, sir."

Jack held up a length of chain. "A choke collar."

"Yes, please." Just the sight of the silver chain that he knew would dig into his throat had his cock weeping with pre-cum.

Jack fastened the metal dog chain around Corey's neck. It was cold on his skin. "That looks fabulous." It was the type of choker collar used to train big dogs, but it didn't have the metal studs to poke the neck, just the chain that slid through a loop, but it would choke him enough if Jack tugged on it.

Corey didn't think he'd actually use it. Jack had been way too afraid of hurting him since he'd drawn blood.

A flick of the quirt stung his other thigh. The double strips of leather slapped together and bit his skin when they connected.

Corey's pulse raced, and he could imagine the metaphorical barbed wire relaxing as his heart pounded freely for the first time in weeks. Yes, he needed more. "Use it," he whispered, thinking of the choke chain.

"Shush now. Unless you're using safe words, no talking."

"Gag me. Please." Corey wanted to feel utterly helpless.

Another sting of the viper lashed his thigh, higher up than the last time. Corey wondered what that leather sting would feel like across his cock and balls, but he doubted Jack would ever do that. The perilous quirt could easily cut into fragile skin. "More, more," he heard himself begging.

Jack stood back at the drawer, digging through the contents. What next? His cock bobbed happily, waiting for whatever Jack would give him.

"I don't want to gag you right now, Corey."

He heard himself whimper. He wanted it all.

Jack turned around with a cock ring in his hand. Corey swallowed hard. He was on the verge of coming already with just thinking about being gagged and whipped with his nipples stinging from the clamps. Hell, if Jack were to gag him and snap that viper at him a few more times, then one good tug on the choke chain would probably have him shooting across the room. He was so excited about the thought, his cock twitched.

Jack slid the ring over his dick, pushing it snug to the base. Corey groaned and shifted his hips, wanting attention.

"Spread your legs as wide as you can, Corey."

He did as he was told.

"Farther, come on."

Corey pushed his legs out until his weight was held suspended from the hook above his head and his toes were barely gripping the floor.

The viper cracked between his legs, catching the insides of his thighs with the two leather tongues of the quirt. He wanted it on his cock, but couldn't quite bring himself to ask for it. "Oh, God, do it, Jack, please."

"You're very vocal tonight."

"I want...I want it." His head thrashed back and forth. Sweat broke out on his forehead.

Jack chuckled and yanked on the chain between the nipple clamps, sending hot lightning streaking down into his groin. Corey gasped and his eyes rolled, his lashes fluttering against his cheek. The viper cracked again, stinging the outside of one thigh and then the other. Jack made his way down his calves and then back to the insides of his thighs.

"Corey? You with me?"

"Y...Yes."

"Good. Can you say yellow?"

"N...No. More."

"Fine," Jack said with some type of resignation.

There was a moment of silence in the room. Corey slowly opened his eyes. Jack stood right in front of him, so close Jack's collar bone was hovering just out of reach of Corey's lips and tongue. Then he felt it. Jack pulled the choke chain.

"Ahhh..." Corey felt it through his entire body. If he didn't have the cock ring on, he would have come from that pull alone. He couldn't breathe and the chain dug into his skin. Then, the pressure released and he pulled in a big gulp of air.

"You okay, Corey?"

"Yes, God, yes."

"Want to say yellow, now?"

"No. No. M...More. Do it again." He realized he'd brought his legs in together, shifting them back and forth.

He felt Jack's warm hand on his dick, jacking him off slowly. Every few seconds, he'd give a pull on one of the chains, either the one at his nipples or the one at his throat. Corey was moaning wantonly. He couldn't get enough; his skin tingled needing even more.

"Do you want to come, Corey?"

"N...No. More pain." Corey wondered if Jack could heighten his sensations to the point that he shot his load even with the cock ring on.

"You want more?" he asked incredulously.

"Yes, yes, please." Corey watched Jack walk back to his toy chest.

He rummaged through it. "Do you want me to tear up your ass, Corey?"

"Yes, please."

A moment later, Jack pulled Corey's arms down from the hook, but left them cuffed. "Hands and knees on the floor, here." Jack pointed to a spot on the floor between the bed and the whipping wall. He guided Corey there with the choke chain, jerking it around a little. Each flick of the chain made his cock jerk right along with it.

Jack came around to his front and held up a butt plug in front of his face. This one was bigger than any they had used before. It had leather strips hanging off of it like a tail. "Ready for this? Or will you say yellow?"

Corey thought about it for just a second. "Yes, please." He wanted to know what that monster felt like in his ass.

"Do you want me to actually use the lube or just shove it in dry?" Jack's voice was sarcastic.

"Jack?" Corey questioned. He didn't like the sound of where Jack was going. He needed to know they were on the same page.

"Yeah...it's okay, Corey. I'm using the lube." He turned away, but his voice had been softer, sadder.

"Are you okay, Jack?" That was the first time he had ever questioned his Dom, but he needed to know he was safe, or he really would have to stop.

"I'm okay, baby. Give me a second."

"Okay."

Jack had slipped out of the Dom role in the middle of a session. Corey was confused, but he stayed still, willing himself not to squirm. He was still so close to the zone with the sting of the viper still on his thighs and his nipples aching from the clips. He swallowed hard, suppressing his urge to beg.

The choker was tugged again. "Okay. Last chance to say yellow, Corey."

"Please..."

"Please what?"

"Please do it. Please! Don't make me wait." The few minutes he waited patiently had only heightened his need.

The cool gel-covered plug pressed against his hole. Corey pushed back, wanting it, but Jack had not taken any time to stretch him. It slid in, warm pain burned around his ring of muscles. He moaned and settled as he got used to the feel.

"Wiggle your butt, Corey."

He did as he was told and was rewarded with the leather straps swishing across his butt cheeks.

"Oh, damn. That's sexy. Too much."

Jack circled around and stood in front of Corey. He peeled his shorts down his muscular thighs and dropped them on the floor. His cock was sticking straight out. "See what you do to me? You sexy thing."

He stepped forward, grabbing Corey's hair to lift his head and rubbing the head of his cock across Corey's cheek and lips, smearing pre-cum across Corey's face. Corey snaked his tongue out, licking the tip as Jack slid his cock around his face.

"You want this?"

"Yes, yes." Corey's lips brushed Jack's cock as he spoke.

Jack's cock slid between his lips and pulled back out slowly. Corey licked at it. "Yes. Give me your mouth, Corey."

Corey opened his mouth wide, and Jack slid in again. He snapped his hips, thrusting his cock deep into the back of Corey's throat. This was normal foreplay for them, but Corey's hands were still cuffed and Jack pulled a little at the choker chain, making it more intense, cutting off his air, so he struggled to breathe.

"I can see the leather thongs slapping your ass while I fuck your mouth, Corey." He continued pumping in and out. Corey sucked and licked at Jack's cock on each stroke. Jack started moaning. "You are so hot. Fuck, Corey." He grunted and exploded down Corey's throat, Corey swallowing as much as he could. He waited there for a moment, running his hands through Corey's dark hair and humming softly.

When he finally pulled back, Jack jerked the collar again. "Ready for some more, Corey?"

"God, yes, please."

Jack moved behind him and tugged at the butt plug, making Corey moan. Jack smacked his ass with something flat, a paddle. This he was familiar with. The leather tails of the butt plug swished his butt cheeks with every smack. "Enough, Corey?"

"No. More."

The next slap had a bite to it. "This side has studs. Do you like it?"

"Yes, more."

"Yes, more what, Corey?"

"Yes, more, please, sir."

Jack chuckled a little as he slapped Corey's ass with the studded side until Corey was crying out with each smack. Tears were stinging his eyes. "Enough, yet?"

Corey panted. Did he want more? His cock was throbbing. Jack leaned over into his face. He reached under and tugged the chain hanging between his nipples. Corey gulped, fighting for air. His entire body was on fire. He wanted the pain, but he wanted to fuck even more. He decided to give in. "Yellow," he gasped.

Jack stood up. "What?"

"Yellow. Jack. I need..." he groaned. "Fuck me. Please. I need to come." His voice was barely more than a moan.

Jack slowly pulled the plug out of his ass. He reached underneath Corey's body and slid the cock ring off making Corey whimper.

Corey heard the lube click open and in another moment, Jack's cock pushed inside. The butt plug had already stretched him enough, but he didn't care if it hurt; he wanted the hurt. "Fuck me, Jack. Hard, please, sir."

Jack stroked in and out and then pulled out completely. "Turn over. I want to see you."

Corey turned over, and Jack pushed his knees up to his chest. "Fuck, you are hot. Can't believe I'm already hard for you again, Corey." He pushed his cock back inside Corey's hole, rolling his hips. As he found his rhythm, Jack reached down and grabbed a hold of the chain clamped to his nipples, making Corey call out as he yanked it.

Jack brushed across his prostate with every plunge. His nipples were screaming as Jack tugged on the chain. His lower back and butt burned where the new welts rubbed back and forth on the carpet. His senses were on another level with pain and pleasure rolling through every nerve ending. Finally, he felt the float.

Jack grunted with a loud exhale as he released inside of Corey. As he felt Jack's seed squirt, it pushed Corey over his own edge. Just as he stared coming, Jack grabbed the choker chain again. Corey's cock shot out in hard streams, he thought would never end.

As Corey's body shook, Jack crawled up his chest and kissed his face, his cheeks, his eyelids, his forehead, and finally his lips. Corey smiled. He felt sated, exhausted.

"You okay, baby?"

"Mm. Yeah."

"Let's clean up and get in bed, huh?" He slid his hands down and released the nipple clamps.

Corey opened his eyes and looked up at Jack. "That was really good."

Jack stood up and reached down to help Corey up. "Yeah. I think I've got this figured out now."

After a quick cleaning, Jack pushed Corey into the bed and wrapped up with him. In Jack's arms, Corey let himself drift off, feeling very satisfied and somewhat hopeful.

8 Endeavor

Corey woke up curled against Jack, his nose cuddled in that warm spot where his arm met his back. The light hair tickled Corey's nose. It was earlier than he normally woke and the room was still dark.

He kissed between his lover's shoulder blades and rested his hand on Jack's hip. The welts on his thighs stung and his ass ached inside and out. He shifted his hips in an effort to get comfortable, wanting to enjoy a few minutes of cuddling against Jack, but he didn't want to wake him up with his tossing around. Finally, he propped his knee up on Jack's thigh, and tried to relax into his pillow.

"You okay, baby?" Jack asked as he turned to face Corey.

Corey settled his knee back up on Jack's leg after he turned. "No," he whined. "These welts are stinging."

"The viper bites, huh?" He wiggled his eyebrows at his little joke.

Corey buried his face in Jack's chest. "Yes," he muttered against Jack's hot skin.

Jack's hands ran over Corey's shoulders then dove into his hair. Jack kissed his forehead and then sat up, leaving Corey to push himself back to his own pillow. "Lay on your back." Jack snapped on the lamp on the side table.

"I can't," Corey groaned. His ass hurt too much.

"Why? Oh!"

Corey rolled over on his stomach and spread his legs,

feeling incredibly needy, as Jack dabbed the anti-bacterial ointment on the red slashes along his thighs, easing the sting. He didn't mind the ache of the spanking, but it felt like his thighs had been slashed open. It was a little much, even worse than the single tail tearing up his back. He hummed as the ointment took the sting away a little.

"Damn, I'm so sorry, Corey." Jack's fingers were light on the back of his thighs.

"Why?"

"I don't like hurting you like this."

Corey laughed into his pillow, then turned on his side, pulling away from Jack's touch. He couldn't hide his smile. "It felt so damn good. I know what I'm asking for."

"I don't like the after effects much."

"I don't like the stinging cuts. The rest of it? Hmm..." He let his head lull back as he fell into a blissful state.

"Damn, Corey, that's hot."

"I'd ask you to spank me again right now—"

Jack cut him off with an adamant, "No!"

"Yeah, but I said it."

"What?"

"Yellow," he giggled. "Now get back up here and reward me."

Jack dropped the ointment back on the nightstand and crawled over to Corey, pulling him up against his chest. He smothered kisses on his forehead and cheeks. "You did, didn't you?"

"Yeah."

Corey nuzzled against Jack's chest feeling replete and well loved. Living with Jack was turning out to be a dream. He wondered why he had killed himself making the decision. Why didn't he just do it instead of wasting all that time? That was past, and he wanted nothing more than to enjoy the moment and look forward to the future. "Jack, I don't think I've ever been happier."

"Good." Another kiss on his head. Jack's hand warmed his shoulder. "I want you happy. I love you, baby."

Corey kissed Jack's chest. "Love you, too." He couldn't think of a better time or way to exchange those words. He'd thought he loved Jack for a while, but admitting it out loud felt good, especially since Jack had said it first.

They lay there for a few minutes enjoying the quiet morning. The light seeping through the cracks in the window treatments sent deep orange and rust beams across the walls. The artwork seemed to dance with the colors, changing as the sun slowly rose. Maybe this thing could work out after all.

"Corey? How's the job thing coming along?" His words were tentative, but Corey didn't mind the question. It felt like Jack was only probing out of concern, not being his usual control-freak self.

"Not bad actually. I had a couple of interviews last week. One was with Dare Records. That would be so cool, but there's no advancement."

"That's something to think about."

"Uh-huh." Their voices in the early morning felt comforting like the normal conversations married couples would share. It was the easiest Corey had felt with Jack since they'd first started dating. Between the lovely romantic dinner and the pain-play afterward, they both seemed more relaxed. Corey's regularly bound heart felt free.

"What was the other interview?"

"Just a file clerk. Crap job. The company is good though with a lot of advancement and very LGBT friendly. I could get my C.P.A. while working my way up."

"Sounds like a plan, but why don't you just get your certification. I'd pay for it."

"No. I need to do this on my own, Jack."

"Fine. I'll let you do it your way, but I'm more than happy to help, if you ask."

Corey leaned up and gave him a quick kiss on the lips. He couldn't believe Jack had given in so quickly. "Thank you." He rubbed his thumb across Jack's bottom lip. It was full and red, thicker than his upper lip that dipped down in the center. He wanted to lick at those perfect lips.

"So, what company is that?"

Corey cringed away from Jack. He didn't want to say, but he knew the more he withheld the worse it would be. "Apex," he said, trying to sound casual.

"What?"

"I know what you're going to say."

Jack sat up fast. Corey's head fell back on the mattress. "Really, Corey? Why don't you just come work for me?"

"I can't do that."

So much for their peaceful morning. Jack was going to get bent out of shape. "Well, you can't work for motherfucking Apex either. Apex Realty? Really?"

"It was just an interview, Jack. They haven't offered me anything. Yet."

"Fuck. I'm offering you something. Come work in our file room. Hell, scrub the floors for all I care, but do not insult me by working for Apex." He thumped his fist into the mattress.

"Okay, Jack." Corey's voice sounded firm. He was proud of that.

"Okay, what? You won't work for them or you'll come to Wolfe?" Jack's company was Wolfe Triple Net and Real Estate Investments and the number one competitor for Apex on the Real Estate side of things. Jack had built his company from the ground up. Apex was completely different, part of a huge conglomerate. Hell, it wasn't even their Real Estate division that he'd applied to, but it wouldn't do much good telling Jack that.

"I'm not working at Wolfe. I can't work for you, Jack." Corey looked up into Jack's face, his eyes smoldering in the early light. "I won't work for Apex, either. If they even make me an offer, I'll turn it down. Promise."

"Seriously, Corey. If you'd just go ahead and get your CPA you could work anywhere. Right? This would be so much easier. I'll pay for whatever you need."

Corey sighed heavily. "No. You won't."

Jack jumped off the bed, snatched a pair of athletic shorts out of his drawer, and stormed out of the room. Corey lay there with his aching ass and the remnants of Jack's wrath tearing up his heart. Maybe they didn't really love each other. Maybe they just wanted to call it love because they couldn't admit what it really was.

He could hear Jack banging around in the kitchen. He knew he should get up. They couldn't leave the argument like that. Finally, when the coffee aroma filtered back to the master bedroom, Corey stirred. He stopped in the guest room to grab a pair of boxers and finger comb his hair.

Jack was in the kitchen leaning over the counter, his arms spread wide. His face contorted as he worked though several emotions.

Corey sat down quietly at the dining room table, tucking one foot underneath him and waited until Jack brought him a mug of coffee.

"I'm sorry, baby," he said, setting the mug in front of Corey.

"Me, too." Corey took a sip of coffee, black with just a little sugar, perfect.

"I won't get all in your job hunt, if you just don't go work for Apex, okay. Settled?" Jack stood beside him and ran fingers through Corey's hair.

"Yes."

"I just want one thing in return."

Corey's heart started pumping. When Jack wanted something from him, it was either going to be incredibly sexy or start another argument. "What?" He held his breath.

"I want to introduce you to my club. Properly."

"What's that mean?"

The sexy smirk on Jack's face told him more than he wanted to know. This time, Jack's desires would be both incredibly sexy and start an argument. Corey put his coffee on the table and clasped his hands in his lap. He forced himself to be still, but his leg twitched wanting to bounce.

"It means I want to show you off. Present you."
"To your BDSM group?"
"Yeah?"

"How exactly?"

Jack leaned back against the breakfast bar that separated the kitchen from the dining room. "You'll wear something fetish. Leather, probably. And you'll be in submissive role. I'll set you up in the center of the room. Maybe spank you a little. That's all. A little show so everyone will know what I have."

"Like a possession." Corey made it a statement, rather than a question. He understood exactly what Jack was saying.

"Yes, but only for the party. You know I think much more of you than that," he pleaded, hopefully.

Corey didn't know if he believed that. Jack dressed him, fed him, housed him. Like a kept man—a possession. "You really want this?" He didn't understand it, but he didn't understand why he needed the pain either. He submitted to Jack to get what he needed, this was just one more thing.

"Do you?" Jack asked, as if it mattered. Maybe it did.

Corey thought about it and realized his cock had gotten harder and harder the more Jack talked about it. The thought of others watching him, half naked, playing with Jack as Jack's sub, made his blood tingle. The submissive in him did want to please his Dom. Instead of answering, Corey pushed his chair back a little and flipped the front of his boxers down. His hard cock stood right at attention for Jack to see.

"How rude at the breakfast table, Corey." For a moment, he sounded totally serious. Then, Corey watched as Jack licked his lips, his eyes going dark, and he knew Jack was ready to play.

Corey teased, "How about you have my sausage for breakfast, Jack?"

"Bold, Corey."

Jack's cock was tenting out the front of his athletic shorts. Corey was getting to him, and the thought had him giddy enough to start squirming in his seat. Before Corey had a chance to think of anything else to say, Jack tossed his leg over Corey's thighs, straddling him in the chair. He rolled his hips, rubbing his dick into Corey' groin.

"I want you to fuck me right here, Jack, right now," he

panted.

"That can be accommodated." Jack stood up and moved Corey's coffee mug off of the table. Then he pulled Corey up and with a quick twist, he shoved him against the table, pushing his chest against the flat surface. "Grab the edges of the table."

Corey did as he was told. Even without the signal, he knew Jack had slipped into his Dom role, and at the moment, Corey was happy to slide into his own submissive persona.

Jack jerked Corey's hips back away from the table, and pulled his boxers down, then kicked Corey's legs apart leaving the boxers wrapped around one ankle. He ran his fingers down Corey's spine, making him squirm with goose bumps. "Damn, you look good like this. How bad is your bottom, Corey? Tell me the truth."

"Do you want to spank me?"

Jack barked at him with his full on Dom-voice, "Answer my question, Corey." When Jack used that tone, Corey felt compelled to obey and that sent delicious tingles through his belly.

"It's not too bad, as long as you don't use anything studded."

"Mmm." Corey listened as Jack went down the hallway. He couldn't see from where he was stretched out across the table, but he didn't dare move. He tried to keep still, but he couldn't. His body thrummed with anticipation and his leg shook uncontrollably. He had to move something to ease the tension.

A few minutes later, Jack returned. He put his hand on Corey's lower back then rubbed along his bottom. He dropped something on the breakfast bar, but Corey couldn't see what it was. Wondering what Jack was going to use sent a shiver down his spine.

"There's a little bit of bruising, Corey." Jack sounded concerned.

"I don't care." He loved the lingering ache and wanted more.

"Fine. I'll avoid those spots."

"You don't have to."

"Be still, Corey. You don't know—hell, you'd probably end up killing yourself. You have to be able to say no, baby."

Corey didn't answer. He wanted fucked, not an argument. He'd damn well say no when he damn well meant it, but right now was not the time.

"Fine," Jack huffed. "You've been very disrespectful at this table, Corey." Jack's words were gruff, but that only made Corey smile wider.

"Yes, sir."

The first smack made Corey jump. It was hard, but didn't sting too bad. It felt like just a flat paddle. The second smack hit his opposite cheek, then back to the first. Corey settled in and his body stilled. Jack smacked several more times going back and forth between butt cheeks and sending Corey into a calming blissful state, but then he landed on one of the bruises, and Corey almost jumped off the table with a shout.

Jack put his hand on Corey's back to comfort him. "Sorry, baby."

"It's okay."

They stayed like that for a moment. Corey's breaths slowing back to normal. "You do look so good like this. Pretty pink ass. I want to take a picture."

Corey's head lurched. Something about taking pictures of him in such a vulnerable state pushed his mind right over the edge. He called out, "Red. Red! No, no pictures."

Jack laughed. "I was kidding, babe, but nice to know you do have a limit. That red was just for pictures, right?"

Corey groaned. He needed to be fucked so desperately. "God, yes." He started panting again. "Please, Jack. Fuck me now."

Corey felt a lubed finger slide down his crack and into his hole. He hadn't been paying attention. He squirmed at the feeling and bucked his hips back.

"Be still." Jack's hot palm rested on the small of his back, probably in an attempt to calm or center him, but he was having none of that. He wiggled around, hips digging painfully into the table.

"Oh God, Jack," he moaned as Jack slid a second finger in and twisted it around, stretching Corey out a bit. "Just fuck me now." He didn't care if he was ready or not, he relished the burn.

"You're very mouthy today, Corey," Jack said, sounding a little aggravated.

Jack's fingers slid out, leaving Corey wanting more. He rolled his hips, feeling so depraved. It seemed an eternity before Jack's hands grabbed him and his hard cock breached Corey's hole, forcing a loud moan out of his mouth. "More, more, please."

"Shh. Don't make me gag you, Corey." Jack drew back and then slid his cock in hard, all the way. Their bodies locked together. Corey trembled, his whole body quaking with the closeness and his need.

"Jack," he cried out.

Jack pulled out completely, leaving Corey empty.

Corey lifted his head to look over his shoulder. "Jack, no, please." Jack turned away and headed to the master bedroom. "Jack?"

"Be still, Corey." In a moment, he came back and stood next to the table at Corey's head. "Open," he commanded.

Corey opened his mouth and Jack stuffed a red ball in it. It tasted like plastic. Leather straps attached to the ball on either side at Corey's cheeks. Jack pulled them back and fiddled with them, adjusting and fastening them together at the back of Corey's head.

Corey felt his cock jump. They'd talked and teased about the gag, and Corey knew it was in Jack's toy collection, but he had never used it. Corey suspected Jack was afraid to use it because it was hard enough, if not impossible, to get Corey to use the safe words. If Jack gagged him, he would certainly not be telling him to stop. Corey wiggled around almost involuntarily at the happy thought.

"Okay, be still now." Jack chuckled; the sound felt like

bubbles swelling up in Corey's chest. "You brought this on yourself, mouthy-boy."

Corey didn't think he could be more turned on. His hands gripped at the edge of the table. His tongue pressed against the ball in his mouth, and his ass was in the air, begging Jack to take him.

"Okay, now, slap the table if you need to stop. And Corey...don't you dare come until I let you. I don't want to use the cock ring this morning."

Corey nodded, unable to answer verbally.

Jack slid his cock back into Corey's hole, and Corey pushed back to meet his stroke. Corey concentrated on the feel of Jack sliding in and out, his hand on Corey's hip, and the smooth texture of the gag against his teeth. He wasn't sure he'd be able to hold back with his prostate being kneaded by Jack's thick cock on every stroke, whipping him up into a frenzy. Corey pressed his tongue against the gag and made mewling sounds around it as he writhed against the table.

He felt the hot spray as Jack came inside him with a "Hah!"

Corey tried so hard not to come that tears came to his eyes, burning the corners. He was so damn close, dancing on the edge.

"Don't. Hold it, Corey," Jack called out, as he likely knew his orgasm would throw Corey over the edge.

Jack pulled out. Corey's body was shaking from head to toe. He felt Jack's hand on his shoulders and hip, flipping him around and shoving him farther up on the table. The wood was hard and cold against his back. His knees bent around the edge.

Jack's mouth came down around his cock, taking him in to the base. Fingers brushed at his balls, as Jack sucked up and down. Corey moaned loudly, not knowing how he was holding back. He needed Jack to release him. His mind and body lingered in a suspended state between bliss and torture. Nothing else existed in the world, but Jack's hot mouth.

Finally, Jack stood up. Looking down into Corey's eyes,

he smiled seductively, proudly. "Okay, baby. Come now for me." His fingers flitted around the tip of Corey's cockhead. "Now," he said again forcefully, and Corey jerked up as he released, shooting out into the air, over Jack's fingers, and all over his chest.

Jack pulled Corey's limp body off the table and into his arms. Corey's body continued to tremble and he felt hot tears leaking out of his eyes. Jack kissed his face, forehead, eyelids, and the top of his head. He pulled Corey's face into his chest and worked the straps of the gag loose. "You were so good, baby. So, good. How can you not understand that I want to give you everything?"

The gag came out, and Corey shut his mouth, relaxing his tight jaw. He made a soft humming sound and rested his head against Jack's chest. He settled down with Jack's arms around him, keeping him warm. It felt like home.

"You make me so happy, baby." He pulled back and kissed Corey's lips, ever so gently. "You okay?"

Corey nodded.

"Good." With another kiss, he set Corey up on his feet. "Go take a shower, and I'll get us some breakfast."

Corey nodded again, and headed for the shower on shaky legs.

Corey and Mick set the groceries on the kitchen counter. "Thanks, man. I got it from here," Corey said, dismissing him.

"You sure?"

"Of course. Go on. Thanks again!"

"All right. See ya later." Mick left, and Corey started putting the groceries up. The driver sure as hell didn't have to help him bring the bags up, he wasn't going to have him help put shit away, too. Jack tended to ask too much of him anyway.

"What took you so long?" Jack asked, getting his attention.

"Long? I didn't think it was that long. Look. I found some great fresh fruit."

"Great. Did you pick up salad stuff and chicken?"

"Yes. And steak."

"What?"

Corey froze. He lifted the steak up off the counter. "It'll be good."

Jack shook his head. "That wasn't on the list Corey. You don't want to eat too much red meant. And carbs? We are *not* having potatoes with that."

Corey liked steak. "Why not? I'll just work out more the next day."

Jacked huffed and took the steak from him, putting it in the freezer. "Maybe for a special occasion."

"Whatever." Corey rolled his eyes behind Jack's back. "Got your brandy."

"Good boy." Jack kissed him on the forehead and took the brandy and went into the other room, leaving Corey to finish putting up the groceries. "Next time stick to the list," he called out from the other room.

Sometimes he wanted to scream. What the hell was a list good for if you couldn't get things that weren't on them? Corey finished up in the kitchen and made his way into the living room where Jack was stretched out on the couch.

He bit at his bottom lip, not sure what to do. He wanted to join Jack on the couch, but wasn't sure if it was allowed. Maybe he should go back to his room. He stood there, frozen in his indecision.

"Come here, Corey," Jack said.

Corey walked in and stopped in front of the couch. Jack pulled on his wrist, gently coaxing him to the floor between his legs. Corey leaned back against the couch and Jack ran his fingers through Corey's hair, petting him. Those fingers felt good massaging his scalp and carding through his hair, but it also created a hollow place in his chest. Was this normal affection? Corey didn't know.

"Do you want to watch a movie?" Jack asked. That wasn't

something they did together often, but he was okay with that. Jack picked something out, then pulled Corey up on the couch with him. The cuddled back and watched the movie, but Corey wasn't interested in it and started nodding off.

"Corey?"

"Huh?" he jerked awake.

"Why don't you go in the guest room and sleep? I'll wake you when I'm ready for bed."

"Oh, okay." Corey felt like he'd been dismissed like a child. Jack was content to treat him like a doll. Come here, do this, watch this movie. But, it'd been boring, so now he was sent to his room. What could Corey really do or say?

He shut the door and climbed up on the day bed. He hated this room and its forced isolation. If he wanted to stay with Jack, he'd do as Jack said. They pretended that wasn't the case, but it still felt like it was there to Corey.

Maybe he was just overly tired. He closed his eyes and snuggled into the pillow. Jack would wake him soon enough. When morning came, Corey woke up in the spare room. Jack had already left for the day. He'd never woke Corey up. They'd slept alone, and Corey felt like he'd been punished, but he wasn't sure what he'd done wrong.

Jack had left a note by the coffee pot that said he fell asleep on the couch and didn't want to wake Corey in the morning. He also left instructions for what he should do today and several links to jobs he should apply for. Corey sighed. This wasn't what he'd expected when he'd moved in, but he should have. He shook his head and poured a cup of coffee. He'd better get the day started.

9 Exhibition

Jack was so excited. He'd been getting ready for Corey's premiere for two weeks. It'd taken him some time to pick out exactly what he wanted Corey to wear. He wasn't sure he could get Corey to do it, though, so he needed a significant backup plan. The party was coming up quick and he needed time to convince Corey. He had seemed excited about it when Jack first told him, but as the date grew closer, he became more and more skittish. He was probably nervous, but Jack would reassure him.

They'd easily agreed to no photos and all cell phones would be confiscated at the door. They also agreed on no touching. Corey didn't want anyone else's hands on him, and Jack agreed with that completely. His jealous streak wouldn't allow it. The only thing left to agree on would be what Corey would wear.

He knocked on Corey's bedroom door. "Yeah?"

Pushing it open, he got a good look at his lover. The light of the computer screen highlighting the shadows of his face, making his cheek and jaw bones seem more prominent. His eyes flashed with curiosity. Jack's heart started pumping like he'd just run five miles on the treadmill. Corey's beautiful face, such a mixture of innocence and lust, continued to have a powerful effect on Jack. "Hey, lover. Want to take a break?"

Corey still hadn't landed a job, but Jack didn't really care. As long as he was not working for Jack's competitors, everything would be fine.

Corey followed Jack out into the living room. "What's up, Jack?"

"Got a present for you. I want you to wear this at the party." He dropped the bag on the glass coffee table and plopped down into his white leather couch. Corey knelt on the floor at his feet and grabbed a hold of the bag, slowly peeking in. He pulled out a hand full of leather.

"Uh, what is it?"

Jack helped separate the straps and lay them out showing Corey how they would circle around his back and chest. "These will show off all that gorgeous muscle you've been building." He wagged his eyebrows at Corey and was rewarded with shy smile.

Corey picked up the last piece of leather and looked up at Jack, questioning. "What?"

"It's a cock strap. It goes around your dick." The red flush that crept across Corey's face made Jack's cock start to thicken. "You can do this for me, Corey."

"This is it? I don't know." He stuffed the leather straps back into the bag.

"I want to show you off."

"Don't you think that's a little too much showing off? I thought you'd at least give me a jock strap to cover my, uh, parts?"

"I don't want to cover your parts. I want them to see what's mine, what I have, and what they don't—all of it."

"I don't know if I can do this." He covered his face with his hands.

"You can. You are so sexy. I want them to be jealous."

"This feels like a really 'yellow' zone, Jack."

"That's not a no."

Corey shook his head. "I'll think about it."

Jack smiled as he watched Corey walk out of the room. He carried the bag with him. Jack hoped that was a good sign. He really wanted to see Corey all trussed up in leather straps, especially the one around his cock.

There was less than an hour to wait for his guests to arrive and Corey was still in his bedroom with the door shut. Jack had to get him relaxed and comfortable, or this wasn't going to go well. Jack tapped on Corey's door.

"Yeah," Corey answered, sounding more capitulating than welcoming.

Jack pushed the door open and held out the drink he'd fixed. "Rum and coke. A little strong on the rum."

Corey took the drink and sipped at it. "Gah! I needed that." He took another swig, and only then did he make eye contact.

"You look great."

Corey glanced down his body, and Jack hoped he would see what Jack saw. "Okay," Corey muttered.

"So, if it will help, why don't you wear a pair of shorts to start with? Something tight, though. Then, we can do a big reveal. You'll only be exposed for a few minutes. Deal?"

"That sounds so much better." Corey's shoulders dropped and the tension between his eyebrows relaxed. He took another drink, finishing off the cocktail. Jack took the glass back to the kitchen.

A few minutes later Corey walked out wearing the leather straps across his chest and a pair of red shorts. They were silky and open at the legs so he got a good view of Corey's long, defined thigh muscles. The material bulged a bit around his cock, and Jack could almost make out the leather strap wrapped around his partner's dick. "That's really good."

Corey exhaled loudly. "Okay. Maybe I can do this. No touching right?"

"Mine are the only hands that will grace your sexy body, my love."

Corey scrunched up his face and stuck his tongue out. "Better be," he muttered almost under his breath, but Jack caught it. That was Corey's stop. No hands, no pictures.

"Mick will be confiscating cell phones at the door. I asked everyone not to even bring them, but some will try."

"Thanks."

"You look damn good, Corey." He pulled his lover up in his arms, offering reassurances. "Can I put the collar on you?"

"Not the choke collar. You can use the leather one with the lead. I'm okay with that." Corey smiled up at him. Jack rubbed his thumb across his bottom lip. He knew why Corey agreed to the collar and lead. It meant he'd be by Jack's side, protected, the entire night.

Jack was fine with that. "Go get it."

He watched Corey scramble down the hall, his half naked body moving lithely.

The others in his group were going to be extremely jealous, especially Colin Hayward, his ex-Dom. Jack couldn't wait for the look on Colin's face when he got his eyes full of Corey's hot body.

Corey came back into the room and handed Jack the collar and lead. "Can I wear some knee pads? I have a black pair from when I used to ride BMX that are tough looking—all black."

Jack smiled. "My little masochist wants to protect his knees?"

"Please, Jack. I think it'll look hot." He wiggled his eyebrows, making his best lecherous face.

Jack finished buckling the collar and shoved playfully at Corey's shoulder. "Go put them on and we'll see."

In a flash, Corey was back, on his knees complete with pads in front of Jack. Corey was right, they were pretty hot for some reason. Jack clipped the lead to his collar. "I'm going to keep you on your knees all night then!"

Corey's light laughter made Jack relax. He really was going to do this. He pictured how Corey would look, standing on the platform they'd set up in the center of the living room, with the leather straps across his back and around his hard cock, and the knee pads on. The visual made blood flow into his cock.

"Okay, I'm going to change." He rushed into his bedroom and stripped quickly. His outfit for the night would be simply a pair of leather pants and a loose silky white shirt. No need to take the spotlight from his little toy.

10 Contention

Corey's nerves spiked as the guests started arriving and mingling around the table that had snacks laid out. Jack had catered the food and set the breakfast bar up with a hired man to mix drinks. He'd even set up a tub of ice with beer bottles sticking out at all angles in the kitchen.

Corey tried to ignore everyone and just keep his eyes on Jack's bare feet. He let his Dom guide him all over the house, back and forth and around while attached to the lead. He knew his ass was exposed in the back as his shorts rode up his crack, and he felt their eyes on him. It aroused him and kept him aroused to the point that his dick was tugging against the leather of the wrap. He wondered if his cock might bust out of the snug thing.

He was exceedingly nervous about having his most private parts exposed. When the shorts came off, he knew he was going to be naked, except for the thin leather harness across his chest and back and the thick one around his cock. The head of his penis stuck out the top of it and the leather wrapped around the length of him. Silver snaps held it in place, sticking up above his bare balls, waxed clean at Jack's insistence.

In one aspect, it was totally hot, and the anticipation of it was killing him, but on the other side of that was an almost all-consuming fear. How many times had he had that dream where he went to school naked? That nightmare was about to come true in a very real sense. He didn't know if he could do this, even for Jack.

It was too much like using safe words. He was set up for the pain and humiliation. It was the humiliation part he was having issues with this time. With Jack alone, he'd suffer anything, but with all these strangers watching, it felt a lot more difficult, yet there was no going back at this point. He wouldn't do that to Jack, even if he could.

Jack tugged on his lead, pulling him over to the stereo. Corey followed obediently, knees sliding along in the pads and fingers digging into the lush carpet. Jack changed the music to something soft and classical and turned the volume down low.

Tugging on the lead, he directed Corey back to the center of the living room. Jack had removed all the tables and set up a small stage that was a few inches high, just enough to take a step up to get on it.

All the white leather furniture was pushed back and arranged around the platform. The carpets, the furniture, the walls, and the platform, all done in white contrasted sharply against the black leather Corey wore and his dark hair. Jack obviously thought it splendid, but Corey felt cold, drowning in all that white.

Jack nudged Corey up the step. "Stand up. Good boy."

Corey stood on the platform, with his hands clasped behind his back and his eyes lowered to the floor in front of him, just like he normally would play with Jack. He knew what was coming and he felt the urge to squirm around creep up his body and claw at his skin, but he ignored the sensation and kept still, concentrating on his breathing in an attempt to ignore the discomfort.

Corey swallowed hard as Jack started his speech, still unsure if he could go through with the presentation.

Jack started, "Hello, guests. Thank you for coming by my home this evening. We all know why you're here, so I will keep it short. Let me present my lover and my sub, Corey Roman." He reached over and slid his fingers into the waist band of the shorts and started tugging them down. "You okay, baby? You ready?" he asked softly.

Corey wanted to say no. He felt the heat on his face and sweat gathering at the back of his neck. He nodded briefly and closed his eyes, as if not looking would make things easier.

Even as nervous as he was, he felt his cock grow harder with each little tug on his shorts. He felt the silky material pooling down at his feet, hanging around his ankles, but he couldn't move to step over them. He was terrified, yet excited in one mixed-up ball of emotion. His stomach knotted, he held his breath, and squished his eyes shut tightly.

"Breathe, Corey." He heard Jack's voice, felt his hand against his thigh.

He took slow breaths in and out, trying to stay calm.

"Can I spank you?" he asked.

"Yellow." He needed more time. His voice quivered as he said, "I'm not used to this yet."

"Okay, baby."

Jack let him stand there for a minute. He knew everyone at the party gathered around looking at him, at his ass and his cock, all trussed up in leather. He tuned out the cacophony of their whispers and comments and listened to the soft music in the background.

Jack ran his hands up and down Corey's arms from shoulder to elbow, slowly. "You know I love you Corey. You're so beautiful. So good, such a good boy," he repeated softly, trying to calm Corey. His hot breath rushed over Corey's skin as he spoke.

Corey was ready to bolt like a wild racehorse. If he were going to get through this, he needed the pain. The softness was not working for him.

"Jack? Jack?" He had to say it twice because he could barely hear himself through the rush of blood swishing in his head.

"Yes, baby? Are you ready?"

"Please."

"Does that mean you want me to spank you?"

"Yes, please. Now?"

"Okay, baby. Open your eyes and step down."

Corey stood there frozen. He didn't want to open his eyes. Opening his eyes would make it real.

"Come on baby, just to step down. You have to open your eyes." Jack's voice was too soft, placating. He couldn't listen.

There was a few tense moments of standoff. Jack was leaving it up to him. He could either stand there with his eyes closed while everyone ogled his hard-on, or he could open his eyes and let Jack spank him until he floated above it. Why couldn't Jack just go all Dom and command him? The bastard constantly told him what to do, until he really needed the domination. He hated the softness.

Corey started shaking. He had to do this. Had to do it for Jack. He slowly opened his eyes a crack. He kept his head down.

"That's it baby, step down." He sounded like he was coaxing a frightened animal.

Corey took the step, then closed his eyes and leaned into Jack's side. "You have to be the Dom," Corey whispered, not sure if Jack heard him or not or if he understood what Corey was trying to tell him.

"Over my knee, Corey." The command came in the deep authoritative tone of Jack's Dom. Corey practically sighed with relief and tossed himself over Jack's knees when Jack sat down on the platform.

Jack spanked his ass several times with his bare hands, making it sting. With each slap, Corey slowly relaxed, bit by bit.

"Use this," he heard a masculine voice say.

Then, he felt another sting, harder than Jack's hands. Someone had handed him a paddle. Corey sighed again and felt himself begin to float as the paddle struck his ass and upper thighs. The party around him disappeared.

"Corey? You with me?"

"Yes," Corey opened his eyes.

"Can you stay here on your knees with your hands on the

platform, so everyone can admire your red ass?"

"Yes, sir." Corey planted his knees on the floor and leaned over the low platform. His butt was up in the air and anyone walking by could see it and his hard cock. The strap seemed to be working much like a cock ring. He felt like he was bulging out of it.

"Spread your legs a little more baby."

Corey did as he was told, even though he knew they would all be looking at his balls. He didn't much care anymore. With the pain centering him and knowing that they'd already seen it all, he was fine and still blissed out.

He felt Jack's warm breath in his ear. "You did so good, baby. I'll reward you after the party. I'm going to get a drink. I'll be right back, okay? You want some water?"

"Yes, please."

Corey watched Jack walk into the kitchen. He could hear people behind him, but he was so focused on his Dom and where he was, he didn't pay attention to anyone else. He felt a light touch on the small of his back.

His body jumped. "Don't touch me," Corey said, startled and pulling out of his numb state much faster than he was used to.

The same masculine voice that had spoken up earlier and handed Jack the paddle came from directly behind him. "Sorry, I couldn't resist. You are so fine. I'm sure Jack won't mind if I play a little, considering."

The touch came again only more firm, and stayed on the small of his back. Corey's heart started pounding into the metaphorical barbs surrounding his heart, making it feel as if it would burst open.

"Please. Don't touch me." Corey started to squirm away, his heart pounding furiously as if he'd been working out instead getting worked over.

"Shh. It's okay." The owner of the voice shoved a lubed finger up his ass, grabbing him around the waist so he couldn't escape.

"Red! Jack! Red! Don't touch me!" Corey screamed at the

top of his lungs.

The man let go and Corey fell over the platform smacking his face into the side of it. He ignored the pain and rolled over, so his bottom was solidly on the ground. In front of him, Jack had grabbed the man by his collar and smashed his fist into his face with a loud smack.

"You do *not* touch what is mine!" he roared and punched the man again.

The man fell back on the floor, bleeding onto Jack's white carpet. He wore a sleek gray suit with a red tie that did nothing to hide his muscular build. His dark hair was cut in a business style over his ears. He was about the same height as Jack, maybe a smidge taller, but Jack was barefoot and this guy was wearing a very expensive pair of loafers. Corey wouldn't have been able to get away from the guy on his own.

"Fuck, Jack. I was just playing." The man was on the floor, dabbing at his nose, while two other guys held Jack back.

"Get the fuck out of my house, Colin."

Someone else helped Colin up and shoved him toward the door.

"Damn it. Corey, go to your room and change, please." His words were harsh. Corey felt like his heart had shattered, splintering around the barbed wire, but he obeyed promptly.

By the time Corey had pulled off all the leather and put on slacks and a polo shirt and came out to the living room, most of the guests had left, but not all of them. A young woman around Corey's own age was sitting on the couch. She wore a skimpy, gauzy dress and a leather collar. She winked at Corey and sipped her drink. Several other folks were talking with Jack. "Hey, Corey. Come sit with me," the girl said.

Corey sat down next to her. "Hi."

"Hi yourself. Oh, my name is Jillian."

Corey shook her hand.

"I'm a sub, too. My Dom is Kenneth. The one with the gray around the temples. Over there. In the dark suit." She pointed to the guest across the room.

"Oh." He was old enough to be her father, but Corey was

certainly not about to judge anyone else's relationships as fucked-up as his own was. He thought it would be nice to chat with another sub for a few minutes, but he figured that wasn't going to happen, when a pounding at the door interrupted the rest of the party.

11 Reflections

Hours later, Corey sat on the couch in the living room, wrapping his arms around his shoulders and stomach. Everyone had left, including Mick, who had been very helpful. He'd been right there by Corey's side looking up emergency phone numbers and kicking the guests out and more importantly, keeping Corey from completely freaking out.

Jack was in jail.

Whoever the asshole was that had assaulted Corey pressed charges for assault against Jack for defending Corey. How bitterly ironic.

Corey listened to the silence. He'd been here without Jack before, but this time it was striking, significant. He was truly alone, not just waiting for Jack to get home. His eyes were constantly drawn to the blood stain on the carpet. Jack would be so upset, but he couldn't get the stain out.

He'd taken three showers since everyone had left. He felt so violated and alone. He was as stained as the carpet.

He'd placed his trust in Jack completely, and he'd never been so let down. Granted, Jack punched the guy multiple times, but Jack shouldn't have left him vulnerable to someone who couldn't be trusted, especially with the state of mind Corey had been in. He had been unable to defend himself, protect himself. He felt like a fool. He felt like a loser, unworthy.

Corey thought he was done with tears, but they started up again as if the next round of sharp thoughts cut him physically, making him cry.

Jack's lawyer told him to get some sleep; nothing would happen before morning. He also told Corey to press his own assault charges. There were plenty of witnesses, but Corey didn't know any of them. He didn't even know the bastard's name that started this shit. He'd wait until Jack got out, and do what Jack wanted.

What Jack wanted? That's what led them to this mess in the first place.

Corey leaned over and screamed into the couch cushion.

He couldn't trust Jack anymore. Where did that leave them?

He wanted to call Dirk and go over to his old place, even if it meant crashing on the couch, just so he could feel safe. He couldn't leave the penthouse, though. Couldn't bring himself to leave. Couldn't bring himself to go sleep in Jack's bed, either. He sat on the leather couch, staring at that bloody red spot in the middle of all that pristine white carpet.

He was straddling that zone where Jack often led him between happiness and total failure, bliss and torture. He should be used to it, but this time the razors cut too deep.

12 Havoc

Jack finally walked out of the jail near five o'clock the next day, relieved to see Corey and Mick, his driver, waiting for him. From what he understood, Mick had been very helpful with the emergency numbers and getting his lawyer, Sheldon Taylor, on the case right away. He hadn't been sure about Mick when he first started because he seemed young and inexperienced, but he was turning out to be one of the best hires he'd ever made.

The entire situation pissed Jack off beyond belief. He knew the charges would be dropped, eventually. It was nothing more than a pissing contest that neither he nor Colin would be able to win and he so hated playing these games.

He told Sheldon to just call the bastard and lay it out. Neither of them needed or wanted the publicity that would be inevitable if they drug this thing out. He would love to see Colin behind bars for assaulting Corey, but at least he'd dished out a little punishment to the bastard. The man was scum. How had Jack not realized that his opinion hadn't been worth all of this?

Jack had spent time rethinking his entire relationship with Colin and his own failures with Corey. He worried that he just hadn't learned enough, or perhaps learned the wrong things from the man. How could he respect someone and trust his word when he'd badly breached the trust of a sub.

Corey was sitting on the edge of a plastic chair in the big waiting room at the front of the jail, near the door. Mick stood beside him, biting his nails. When Mick caught sight of Jack, he swatted Corey on the shoulder, making him jump. Corey looked up; his eyes full of tears.

Jack felt like hitting the floor, on his knees. He let Corey down and that was something he considered unforgivable. He froze, not knowing what to do. Corey rushed over and stopped right in front of him, looking up at him with expectation written all over his face.

Jack didn't have an argument for him. "Let's go home," he said as he ushered Corey through the big glass doors.

The ride home in the limo was too quiet. Jack reached out and grabbed Corey's hand and was just happy that he didn't pull it away. For the first time in their relationship, Jack was the one seeking comfort, and he didn't know how to handle it. He despised being self-conscious, insecure, and he hated how much he needed Corey to be there for him.

They were getting close to the penthouse. "I'm sorry," Jack said.

Corey squeezed his hand. What did that mean?

They held hands on the elevator and up to the penthouse door. Corey let them in, and as they stepped inside, Jack said, "I'm glad Mick was there for you."

"It wasn't the same."

"That's not what I meant." Jack followed Corey into the living room. "Damn, I need a drink." The remnants of the party were gone, leaving his home in pristine condition. "Did you clean up?"

"Yeah, I had nothing else to do." He ran his hands through his hair.

"Thank you."

Corey plopped down on the sofa. His face was a stoic mask that Jack desperately needed to see behind.

He poured a glass of brandy and stood on the edge of the living room. "Are you mad at me?"

Corey looked over his shoulder. "Can I have a sip of

that?"

Jack walked around the couch and handed Corey the glass. He sipped it and handed it back. Corey leaned back into the couch and closed his eyes. "I think I'm done."

"Done? With what?"

Corey got up and walked across the living room. He wore gray slacks, Kenneth Cole loafers, and a light yellow polo. He looked like a preppy college kid, clean with a sexy air about him, but his demeanor had sunk right back to the sullen boy he had been before he'd moved in. Jack didn't like that. "Corey?" he asked.

Corey kept walking. He went into the guest room and shut the door. This was bad. Jack didn't know what to do. This was way beyond the Dom/sub relationship. They were broken again.

He set his drink down on the coffee table, wondering what Corey had done with the platform they'd used at the party. Probably burned it. He noticed the blood stain from Colin's broken nose ruining the carpet like a splatter of spite and regret. Nothing to be done about that. He stood up and followed Corey's path down the hall. He needed a shower to get the grime of the jail off of him and a good night's sleep to recharge, but Corey came first.

He paused at Corey's door. He heard sobbing. His heart shattered. He'd done this, hurt Corey, the love of his life, really hurt him. He could blame it on a lot of things, most especially Colin motherfucking Hayward, yet he knew it all boiled down to his own goddamned ego.

He wanted to be the big shot, wanted to show Colin how far he'd come and what a prize Corey was. What, a prize? He was, but not the kind you strapped up in leather and strutted around in front of your colleagues. He groaned at his hindsight and tapped at the door.

Corey didn't answer.

Jack pushed the door open. Corey was face down on the day bed. He'd changed into boxers and an oversized t-shirt. His face cradled in the crook of his arms. "Go away, Jack." His voice was rough from the crying and chipped away at his heart.

"No. Baby. I'm so, so sorry. Can we talk about this?"

Corey sat up and rubbed at his face. His eyes and cheeks were red from crying. "No," he sobbed. "I can't do this. I'm not—I'm not ready to talk to you."

Jack sat down on the day bed next to Corey and put his arm around him. "I'm the biggest ass in the world. I'm so sorry, baby."

Corey started sobbing. He leaned into Jack's shoulder and Jack wrapped his arms around him, pulling him tight, and just let him cry it out.

"Jack? He violated me. You let a stranger put his finger up my ass. Damn it!" He sobbed harder and Jack pulled him close, but this time Corey pushed away. "Get away. Get out. Just leave me alone."

Reluctantly, he got up and went back to the living room and sat down on the couch. He was at a complete loss, stunned, and unable to figure out what he needed to do.

Jack had no idea how long he'd been sitting there before Corey came out wearing a pair of jeans and the same oversized T-shirt. His back pack was slung over his shoulder.

"Fuck, Corey. No. Please. Don't leave me. Don't leave. Give me another chance."

"I don't know. Don't know if I can. I just need some space." His voice was soft and controlled and he didn't look at Jack. He just turned and stormed out the front door.

Jack stood there in the center of his home, staring at the door. His brain unable or unwilling to comprehend that Corey had left. His world had become nothing more than an empty void.

13 Fragments

Corey hated crossing the lobby of Jack's building. He preferred using the garage entrance. It seemed so much less formal, just gray concrete slabs, cold but not unfriendly. By contrast, the lobby was ornate with gold trimming garish on the walls, marble floors and exotic furniture. It felt cold and hostile, despite the richness.

He quickly stepped out through the big glass doors and into the cool evening air. He crossed his arms and looked down the street, waiting for Dirk. His cell phone vibrated in his pocket and he pulled it out to see a text message from Jack: *Where you going? I'm worried.*

That was just like Jack. Corey didn't want him worrying though. He didn't know what else to do. His fingers flew over the keypad: *To my old place. Called Dirk for a ride. Don't worry.*

Dirk pulled up just as Corey hit send. He climbed in the passenger side of Dirk's old Honda Civic and stuffed his backpack on the floor board at his feet.

"You okay, Corey?" Dirk asked as Corey pulled the door shut and buckled the seat belt in place with a loud click.

"Yeah, I guess."

Corey pulled out into traffic. "I told you he'd dump you," Dirk said, sounding mad.

Corey looked down at his vibrating phone. "I left. He didn't dump me. See?"

He held up Jack's latest text message for Corey to see at the next stoplight: *Corey, I need you. Please come home.*

"So, why'd you leave?" Dirk's voice was full of concern.

"I don't want to talk about it." He typed a final message to Jack that he needed space, then turned off his phone.

"Really? What happened?"

"Really. I said I don't want to talk about it." There was no way he was telling Dirk what happened. Not getting into it at all was the only way to go. His friend could not know he'd dressed up like a bondage slut and Jack's friend finger-raped him. No way. Not happening. Corey rubbed his face, forcing his tears back. Hadn't he cried enough?

It was full dark by the time they got to Dirk's apartment. The sky was cloudy and hid the stars making the sky seem untouchable and far away. As he walked in to the apartment where he used to live, he felt like a failure. The barbed wire around his heart had been ripped away, leaving him to bleed out all over his friend's couch.

The next morning, Dirk and his new roommate both got up and left early. Corey heard them mulling around the apartment, but he pretended to still be asleep. He didn't feel like facing them. Didn't feel like facing the world or anyone in it. If he kept his eyes shut long enough, maybe it would all go away.

Finally, his bladder pushed him off the couch. After washing his face and snagging a cup of coffee, he turned his phone back on. There were several text messages from Jack begging Corey to come home and a voicemail message that was probably also from Jack. He didn't even want to check it. He wanted to go back to Jack, but he couldn't. What could he offer Jack now? He felt defiled, useless and so fucked up. He knew it was stupid, but he couldn't quite choke those feelings down. He couldn't go back to Jack when he felt so worthless and violated.

He put his head down face first into the pillow Dirk had let him use. The tears started rolling again. Damn, but he was turning into a girl, for real.

He needed to figure this out, decide what to do, but he felt stuck and so alone in the world, despite Dirk helping him out. Maybe he would call his parents and see if he could go home. That was the last thing he wanted to do. That would mean he failed at life. Thoroughly and completely an utter failure.

Corey cried until he heard his phone ring. He didn't recognize the number. "Hello?" he answered.

"Corey Roman?" the female voice asked.

"Yes, this is Corey."

"Hey, Corey. This is Jillian. Did you get my voicemail?"

"Jillian?" Corey rummaged through his brain, trying to figure out who she was. "I didn't get your voicemail, but I haven't checked yet today."

"That's okay. Listen, I got your number from Jack at the party the other night. Well, before everything went down. He said you're looking for a job." Oh, that Jillian!

"Yeah, I am. Entry level accounting or bookkeeping."

"Okay. Well, I'm a headhunter and I deal with professionals on a higher level, usually. But, I do have a lot of connections. I'll send you my email. Shoot me your resume, and I'll see what I can do."

There was silence on the phone for a minute. "Okay," Corey said. This seemed like legitimate help he didn't want to turn down.

"Uh, you do remember me, right? From the party?"

"Y...Yes."

"Great! I think you're pretty brave. You know? Doing that for Jack. Anyone with that kind of willpower, I can back. I'll call you."

"Thanks."

"Everyone needs a break now and then Corey. You're welcome!"

The phone went dead, but Jillian followed up quickly with a text that had her email address. This could be a good thing and maybe get him back on track, but on track for what, he didn't know.

Corey looked around the apartment at white walls bereft of art work. The couch was at least five years old and the TV had been propped up on a make-shift entertainment center made from milk crates. The only thing in the apartment with value was the game console. He wanted more than that. Living with Jack had ruined him for simple living. Maybe Jillian could help him land a good job and he could move on with his life. He had to email her right away, but he'd left his laptop at Jack's place.

He put his head in his hands, elbows on knees. There had to be an easier way to get through life.

Resigned, he texted Jack: *Will you please have Mick bring my laptop over?*

The return text came quickly: *Yes.*

That was it. Had Jack given up? Corey bit his lip. He really needed to figure out what he wanted. Could he live without Jack? How would he be able to take care of his issues with pain all alone? He didn't know if he wanted to go back to Jack or move on.

14 Assay

Corey looked out the window and saw the long black limousine pull up to the curb. He sighed and went out to meet Mick and get his laptop. Mick got out of the car and came around to the side, but he wasn't carrying Corey's computer. "Hey, Mick. What's up?"

"Good afternoon, Corey." He nodded and then opened the back door. The formal words and empty hands should have given it away, but Corey's breath still caught when Jack stepped out of the car.

Corey cursed under his breath. He crossed his arms over his chest, as if trying to wrap himself up and hide. He stood on one bare foot and put the left on top of the right. He wished he could implode. Heat fired up under his skin with Jack's eyes on him.

Corey scanned him, curiously. He wore a pair of New Balance running shoes, jeans, and a loose white t-shirt, strangely casual for Jack.

"Corey? Are you okay?"

Corey bit down on his bottom lip and jerked his head up and down.

"That's not an answer." Jack stayed by the car. That was good. He couldn't let himself get too close to the man, to smell his scent, to feel his body. No, he needed to keep space between them. It was just safer that way.

"I'm fine. I just...I can't." Corey took a step backwards.

The rough cement of the sidewalk was cold and damp beneath his feet. It must have rained sometime during the night.

"Okay. I'm sorry. I brought your laptop." Jack's voice was soft and unsure. Corey raised his head to meet Jack's stare. His blue eyes were liquid pools, his face solemn. "What do I have to do Corey? I want you to come home." Jack motioned for Mick to get the laptop.

Corey didn't know this Jack, soft and pleading and unsure. He wanted his Dom back, but feared the trust was gone for good.

"I'm broken Jack. I can't...I can't trust you." He took the laptop from Mick and turned to leave. He knew he was running away, but couldn't look back or he might break down. He might throw himself into Jack's arms.

"That's not fair, Corey. Stop!"

Corey stopped. Not because he responded to a dominant voice, but because he was angry. He thought Jack sounded petulant like a child that had lost his favorite toy. "You still think of me as your possession," Corey growled out, turning back to face Jack. "Fuck you, Jack. You let that stranger—just fuck you! I had to deal with all of it alone. Don't you get it? We're done. Leave me the fuck alone!" His voice got louder with each word until the last of it had been screamed. Maybe he wasn't being totally fare to Jack, but that didn't matter as much as his anger in the moment, because that felt a lot better than the empty sadness of being alone or worse, just numbness.

Jack took three long strides to close the distance between them and wrapped his arms around Corey before he had a chance to move away. Damn, his long legs. He shoved Jack's chest, not wanting his touch, afraid he'd give in with Jack so close.

"Damn, Corey. I love you. I miss you. You! Ugh! I messed up. Okay? I'm sorry. I shouldn't have even invited that asshole. Hell, I shouldn't have had the party at all, and I sure as hell shouldn't have pushed you into doing that, when you didn't really want to. I'm sorry. I'm sorry. Please, come home."

Jack's words were obviously heartfelt, but it didn't matter. It was too late. Corey ignored Jack's nose, rummaging through his hair.

"I can't," Corey whispered, pulling away from Jack.

He walked back into the apartment and dropped his laptop on the coffee table. He grabbed the pillow and screamed into it, then threw it across the room. He stood up and paced the floor. He slammed a fist into the cushion of the couch. He walked back to the window. He let the tears stream down his cheeks as he watched the limo pull away from the curb. The best thing that ever happened to him just drove away and left him there in that empty rundown apartment.

His phone vibrated and he picked it up off the coffee table. As expected, Jack texted: *I luv u - this is NOT over!*

Corey fell back onto the couch. He couldn't answer that text. He wasn't sure if Jack really missed him, or missed having someone to push around. Worse, if he were being honest with himself, he wasn't sure if that really mattered to him. He blinked away his tears, determined to distract himself from thinking about Jack. He couldn't stand to face the things he knew he was, the things Jack brought out in him. Physical pain, being controlled by Jack, it came with a price and he didn't know if he could keep paying it.

He scrolled through his contacts, pulling his mother up, instead. He hadn't spoken with her in months, since before he moved in with Jack. His call went to voicemail. "Hey, Mom. It's Corey. Just...uh, I wanted to talk to you. Call you later." He hung up, wondering why he'd even called her in the first place. He was a grown man and had made his own decisions. Now he had to get used to the missing piece of his heart that had been cut out with barbed wire and stuffed into Jack's hands.

Corey sat in the silence, listening to the traffic noises from the street drifting in. He wiped his face with the back of his hand. He knew he had to pull his shattered pieces back together, but his heart was finally and completely shredded. How did he fix that?

His cell phone rang. He checked the caller ID, expecting

it to be Jack, but it was his mother. "Mom?"

"Corey. What's going on? Are you okay?" Her voice sounded far away, or maybe that was just his head.

"No. Uh, I broke up with Jack." There was silence on the other end. His parents hadn't really accepted that he was gay. They hadn't disowned him, but they didn't like to talk about it either. They dealt with it the same way the dealt with anything they didn't like about Corey. They ignored it.

"You sounded down. I thought you might be in trouble or something. When are you going to visit?"

"Mom. Can you pretend I'm talking about a girl or something? Damn Mom! My heart is broken and I just want a little comfort for once."

He heard her frustration as she exhaled. "Seriously, it's been too long. We're busy this weekend, though. Your cousin, Jenny, is working on getting a reunion together for the whole family at the Vineyard next year—"

"Mom. Do you really want me to wait that long?" Why did she always shove him away, even as she tried to pull him closer?

"I'd love to see you sooner, Corey. How long would you want to stay?" He was surprised to hear her say that and wondered if she was holding her breath and hoping he would tell her he wasn't coming.

"I don't know. A few days." He hadn't been home for any extended length of time since he'd left. He'd never had a reason before, and he wondered why he'd thought it a good idea to seek solace from her now. She'd never been very reassuring for him before. Anything but that.

"You're not going to be any trouble are you? I don't think your dad could deal with you hurting yourself or something like—"

"Yeah," he interrupted her, wanting to end that line of conversation with her at all cost. "Bad idea. I can't deal with any of this right now. Maybe I'll call back in a couple of weeks, Ma. My head's not right."

"Whatever you think's best, Corey." She sounded relieved.

"Okay. Love you, Mom."

"Yes, dear. Don't wait so long to call back." Now as they were hanging up, she sounded cheery.

Nothing had changed. He was the bad son for being gay, for not calling, and for finally calling. He couldn't win with her, and his dad was worse. Why had he bothered? His heart wasn't ripped up enough from Jack? They were both just as cold as ever. He wondered how they'd ever managed to get together long enough to actually conceive him. It had obviously been such a horrifying experience that they never repeated it. He couldn't remember ever seeing them kiss or hug in front of him. They turned away when he tried to hug them, either of them. They might love him in their own way, but he couldn't bring himself to care anymore. He didn't have the energy. He shouldn't have called her. When would he learn that they just couldn't be what he needed?

He tossed his phone to the table. It skidded across the smooth surface and bounced to the floor on the other side with a thud. Was there even padding under the cheap carpet? The place smelled faintly of stale beer. Why did he care? What the hell was he going to do?

15 Emanation

Jack rode home in the back of his limo, but it felt like a trash compactor. He'd lost Corey and was clueless as to how to get him back. Jack really didn't do relationships. He was comfortable with Dom/sub, but regular relationships? He'd screwed up every single one, especially this one.

He looked at his phone, flipped it around in his hands, just fidgeting. He tapped in a text and sent it out to Corey.

The car pulled into the parking garage and Mick let him out at the door. "Thanks, Mick."

"Sir, may I say something?"

Jack looked up at his driver. The young man had always behaved in a remarkably professional manner, even when he asked him to do things that weren't in line with being a driver, like helping Corey move and picking up meals, not to mention all the shit he'd helped Corey with when Colin fucked up their world. "Yes?"

"Don't fire me, but you really shouldn't give up on him."

Jack looked down at his phone. Still no return message. "I'm not. I just..."

"So, like, um, when he moved in, it seemed like he was miserable but then up until your party, he was really happy and so were you. Maybe you should focus on that?"

"Do you have a...a significant other?" Jack asked.

Mick shook his head. "No. Yeah, I'll shut up now."

"No. That's not it. You've had them, though, right? Girlfriends?"

"Yes. Just not right now."

"What do I do? How do I get him back?"

The kid's face dropped. He was just trying to make Jack feel better. He was just as clueless as anyone.

"Never mind," Jack mumbled as he turned away.

Alone in the penthouse, all he could think of was Corey. He went to the guestroom and fingered the clothes Corey had left behind, smelling them, wanting to remember his lover in a tangible way, but whether or not his scent lingered in his clothes, it still didn't bring him back.

He sent another text: *I'm lost without you. Please call me.*

He made himself a sandwich for a late lunch but only ate half of it. He poured himself a brandy instead and then called his personal assistant to have her send flowers to Corey. He demanded she have them delivered by the end of the day. He was good at that at least—demanding things.

Jack walked aimlessly around the apartment until he stopped, standing over the bloodstain. He needed to have a professional come in and take care of it or replace the carpet altogether. He stared at the mark for a long time. It felt like the physical embodiment of his pain and he desperately wanted it gone.

His cell rang, and he leapt across the living room. The caller ID said *Taylor, Sheldon*, his lawyer. He answered it immediately. "It's Jack."

"Hey, Jack. It took a little arm wrestling, but Colin said he'd drop the charges if you cover his emergency room bill from that night and a plastic surgeon if he needs it."

"From a broken nose?"

"I know, that's what I said, but he wouldn't budge. Also, no charges against him. Guess that goes without saying."

Jack took a long slow breath. "Corey probably wasn't going to press charges, anyway. Look, I just want it over, so yes. I'll pay. Have him send you the bill, but see if you can put a cap on any future expense. Hell, he wasn't that good looking to start with."

"Gotcha. How's Corey?"

"Don't know."

"What do you mean?"

"He left me. I don't want to talk about it." Jack walked out to the balcony.

"I'm really sorry to hear that. He was good for you."

"Doesn't matter. I blew it." He took a sip of his brandy. "I think he hates me." Jack felt the hot tears burning at the corners of his eyes. "I have to go." He hung up. Sheldon and he went way back; he'd understand.

He set his phone in his lap and drug his hand through his hair and rubbed his face. How had he let things get so out of control?

He picked his phone back up and hit Corey's number on speed dial. As expected, it went to the voicemail, but at least he got to hear three seconds of Corey's voice before he had to leave his own.

"Hey baby, I know you don't want to hear from me, but I wanted to let you know that Sheldon's getting the charges dropped and we don't expect you to have to do anything. No pressing charges or dealing with any of it. Okay? I love you." The message recorder cut off, but he couldn't bring himself to call back.

He sipped on his brandy and looked at the skyline until it started getting dark. He picked up his phone just to head into the house, and it vibrated with a text message from Corey: *Thank you about the lawyer. Stop sending me stuff. I love you, but leave me alone.*

The tears rolled down his cheeks. He really had blown it. He threw the glass of brandy against the sidewall of his balcony, satisfied with the shatter. He'd pay his housekeeper extra to clean it up.

Jack didn't go into work the next day. He couldn't focus on anything at work with Corey dominating his higher functions. He donned track pants and a soft T-shirt and sprawled on the couch, hoping to nap, but mostly just daydreaming about what he might do if he got Corey to come home.

A bang on the door had him jumping. Corey? Few people had access to the building without a call from security before coming up, so it had to be him. He dashed across the suite and flung the door open. "Kenneth?"

The man stood there in a shirt and tie with his sleeves rolled up to his elbows. His slacks were tight, hugging his frame, but in a way that said he was in charge of everything. His hair was styled professionally, a light brown with just a slight amount of salty gray around his temples. Distinguished and dominant must have been what he was going for, because it was working. "Jack. You going to let me in?" His question insinuated that it was a thinly veiled demand.

Jack opened the door. "Right." He motioned for Kenneth to enter. "So, what's up? What brings you here?"

"I wanted to check on you." He strode into the living room like he owned it.

"Me? I'm fine." Jack cocked his head to the side.

"I know. I don't usually check on Doms, but this was... something different. Right?"

Kenneth planted his hands on his hips, daring Jack to disagree with a dark look. Their group didn't have a leader, a president, or anything like that. If they did, it would be Kenneth. He took it upon himself to keep things organized and safe within the group. Jack had always thought of him as the Dom of Doms in his group.

"So? You checking on Colin, too?"

Kenneth gave him a curt nod. "Yes, but this is about you."

"What the fuck?" Jack held his hands up, resigned. What did Kenneth want to know anyway?

"Hey, listen..." He held his hand out. "I'm just checking in to make sure everything's okay. Colin told me you'd resolved the legal issues, but sometimes. Like this..." he said, waving his arm around. "The emotional part of things like this are overlooked, especially with Doms. We're supposed to be tough, together, have the answers. Most of the time, though, we aren't any of those things."

Jack shifted his weight back and forth and crossed his arms over his chest. "I get that. I have more questions now than ever."

Silence lingered in the room for a bit. Kenneth probably expected Jack to offer him a seat, but Jack didn't want the man too comfortable in his home, especially since he'd been the one to barge in. He let that silence linger. It was Kenneth's move.

"So, how's Corey?" Kenneth asked, abruptly.

"I don't know."

"What do you mean? You should be taking care of your sub, Jack."

"He's more than that to me, you know. That's the whole problem. Fucking Hayward. He had no right."

"Maybe you should consider his perspective."

"What the hell does that mean?"

Kenneth sighed and took a step closer to Jack. "He obviously assumed you would share."

"I made the *no-touching* rule very clear." Jack scowled. How could Kenneth ignore that?

"Maybe not clear enough. Colin obviously thought differently. Thought your prior relationship precluded him from your little rule. He took it as a challenge. It's not like you haven't shared with him before."

"I told you, Corey is different." Jack spat the words out in self-defense. Things had been different once before. Colin had been more than willing to share Jack with others when he'd been Colin's sub. That was one of the main reasons he was no longer Colin's sub—that and the fact that he just wasn't a sub.

"So you've said."

"He's my lover, he lives with me. Or he did, until that bastard, Colin—"

"What? Did he leave you?"

"Fuck you, Kenneth. What do you want from me?"

Kenneth plopped down on Jack's couch with a sigh of exasperation. "Damn, Jack. Maybe you should have been bringing Corey around sooner."

"We've been together for over a year and I never heard shit about it."

"But, that's probably why Colin felt—"

"Bullshit!" Jack had to interrupt that line of thinking. "Colin plays that up. He knew better."

"Jack, come now. You know there is a certain expectation set. Everyone shares."

"I'm not sharing. Not Corey. Not with Colin. Not with you." He'd never let Corey go down on his knees for either of them. He'd done it enough to know what it felt like and that was never going to be Corey's role. "Let's just face the facts. Is Colin still in the group?"

"Yes. Of course. We talked about sanctioning him, but really, he's not the one that did anything out of the norm for us."

"Fuck you, him, and the whole fucking group. If he's in, we're not."

"You and Corey? You still speak for Corey when you aren't together?"

"I swear to you here and now, the Dom that goes after Corey is going to have a lot more problems with me than a broken nose."

Kenneth held his hands up. "Hey, wait. I'm not saying that."

"Get off my couch. All of this is bullshit. I said no touching and Colin broke that."

Slowly, intentionally, Kenneth stood up. "I guess I can see how you feel. Though, like I said, you should take just a moment to see it from Colin's perspective."

"No."

Kenneth put his hands on his hips, taking up his power stance once more. "I should have known right away, when we first met, that you'd never be a good sub."

"Colin knew. He knew from our first session." Jack ran his fingers through his hair. "That doesn't solve anything."

Kenneth nodded. "Okay, well. I hope you'll call on me or someone else in the club if you need to talk. Or whatever."

"I don't have anything to talk about unless Colin is out of the picture."

"I doubt he will be, Jack, but I hate to lose you and Corey. You both really need some support right now."

Jack stared at him in disbelief. He would never ask for help, especially from Kenneth and Colin.

"That's what the club is for, Jack. Seriously. If you'd get over Colin and just try to get in deeper with the rest of the community."

"Thanks. I'll keep that in mind." Jack turned and walked back to the front door, opening it wide for his uninvited guest. He offered a fake smile, and nothing more as he waited for Kenneth to leave.

"Okay, Jack. Seriously though. Call me if you need anything. I won't judge you. I won't ever judge you. I know what you've been through with Colin. I've watched you all but self-destruct and then pull yourself back together. I admire that. A lot. So, really. Whatever you need." He held his hand out for a shake, but Jack didn't feel it. He didn't like Kenneth getting all personal and throwing his past out at him when he was at his most vulnerable.

"I meant what I said about the others going after Corey. It won't be pretty."

"I'll make sure they know. Colin included."

"If Colin even thinks about—"

"He won't. I promise you." Kenneth walked out and headed to the elevators. Jack wanted to slam the door, hard, but he didn't. He shut it gently, not wanting to let Kenneth know how deeply he'd gotten under Jack's skin.

16 Anguish

Two weeks later...

Corey just knew he'd blown the interview that Jillian had set up for him; he knew it. He slammed into the bathroom, locking the door behind him. He had no privacy living here. He needed to move on, find his own place, but he was stuck. All he could think about was Jack and going home. *Idiot!*

He had no home.

Jack had stopped calling and texting. He'd given up. Now maybe Corey could move on.

He leaned against the double sink, staring at the adjacent shower. The bathroom was done in a sickly yellow. He hated the cheap linoleum floor and the cheap plastic surround in the shower. He never had a problem with it when he lived here before. It wasn't so much comparing it to what he lost with Jack, but that he'd lost Jack and Jack was the embodiment of finer things.

Hot tears threatened and stung the corners of his eyes just thinking about Jack. He pinched himself in the arm. It wasn't hard enough.

He slid down the counter, letting his ass hit the floor. He let his hand sink into his hair. He pulled. It still wasn't hard enough. His mind kept wandering back to Jack and his choker chain and nipple clamps and butt plugs. He thought about buying some play things for himself, but it just seemed sad and pathetic.

He stood up and rummaged through the drawers until he found a sewing needle. He poured some rubbing alcohol over the entire needle, then took off his shirt. Taking a deep breath and holding it, he shoved the needle into his left nipple until it really did hurt.

Great. He stood there in the bathroom with a sewing needle hanging half out of his nipple.

Fucking pathetic.

He hadn't done anything so stupid in a long time. Since high school. Back then, it'd been the only way to get his parent's attention. It'd quickly become a pattern. He'd act out, yell or scream, get bad grades, and their answer was to ignore it all. Sometimes they would send him to his room, but that wasn't much of a step up from them overlooking him. When it became too much to bare, Corey would find a way to hurt himself. That worked for a while, until they figured it out, then his dad told him if he hurt himself too bad, he wasn't paying the doctor's bill or even taking him to the hospital.

Corey had been desperate, but not stupid. So, he stopped. The last time had been his junior year of high school. That had been a fiasco.

He'd thrown a temper tantrum and his dad had sent him to his room. He stormed through the house, slamming his door behind him. Pacing the floor, he tried to reel in his anger and not let it explode. He growled and screamed and banged his head against the wall, even knowing that it wouldn't do him any good. He'd only be left with a headache and maybe another hole in the wall. He wanted to matter to them; he needed more from them. He didn't understand why he felt that way and wondered for the millionth time why he couldn't just let it all go.

Stopping in the middle of the room, he planted his hands on his hips and held his breath. Something, he had to do something. Light from the neighbor's house shined through the window, catching his eye. Impulsively, he decided to punch his hand through it; shattered glass could not be easily ignored.

Corey had crossed the room with those intentions, but knew he would chicken out at the last minute. He didn't think he was brave enough to actually do it. His heart slammed in his chest and sweat dripped down the back of his neck, chilling at the cool breeze sent through the room by the ceiling fan. Seconds before he reached the window, he did chicken out, but he also tripped on dirty clothes strewn over the floor covering a pair of old sneakers. He fell forward toward the window and stuck his hand out to catch himself. The move was pure instinct, but accomplished exactly what he had wanted. The glass shattered as his hand went through it.

He shrieked at the pain and pulled his arm back toward his body. This instinct managed to slice his wrist across the jagged pieces of the single pain, still left in the frame, sticking up like translucent teeth. Blood dripped down the window and wall, across the floor, down his arm to his elbow. "Mom!" he yelled, voice shaking, on the verge of panic, but not quite there.

Corey's parents had stormed into the room. His mom went in to action, running to the linen closet for a clean towel to press against the cut.

She argued with his father for an hour that they'd be brought up on neglect charges if they didn't do something. The cut needed stitches; it couldn't be avoided. So, they did finally cave and take him to the emergency room, where he ended up getting twelve stitches and eventually a long, ugly white scar that raised up from his skin like a miniature mountain chain. He hated that thing and all that it reminded him of.

He rubbed the vicious scar, still jutting out slightly along his wrist, as he thought about how his parents handled the hospital visit. It'd been his third injury that year and the doctor was concerned, so his parents had told the staff he'd done it to himself. It was the truth and even Corey couldn't deny it, but it only felt like a partial truth. Corey couldn't admit the reality of why he'd done it, hurt himself, this time or any other.

The hospital appointed a social worker and a counselor, and he had stayed in therapy until he graduated from high school and moved on to other things. The therapy hadn't done much, except allow his parent to continue to ignore him, but at least he didn't feel so bad about it.

But he felt bad now. Everything inside of him was threatening to bubble up to the surface, and if he didn't get some kind of release soon, he was going to go crazy.

He pulled out the needle. His god damned nipple was bleeding down his chest. He didn't want the blood, just the pain, otherwise he'd just cut his arm up or something. He scrounged around for a band aid and pulled it across the abused nipple before jumping in the shower. He prepped himself as quick as he could, including lubing up his ass in case he got lucky. He wanted to go out—needed to go out.

He started digging through his backpack; he had nothing decent to wear. He grumbled and decided just to wear what he had already been wearing, crappy jeans and worn out t-shirt. He tucked his wallet in his back pocket and stormed out of the bathroom "Hey, Dirk. I have to go out."

"Out where?"

"You know, OUT-out."

Dirk and his new roommate Stan were eating pizza at the breakfast bar. "Want a slice first? You need a ride?"

"No, no. I'm good." He ran his fingers through his hair. "I just have to go. You know?"

"That's cool, bro. You got money for a couple drinks?"

"No. Where I'm going, I don't need any." Corey shared a fake smile. He knew Dirk would understand, but Stan looked at him funny. He'd let Dirk explain it after he left. "Later." He started for the door.

"Don't forget your cell, and if you need a ride later, call."

"Yes, mom." He tucked his phone in the front pocket of his jeans and headed out.

The walk to the club he wanted to go to was nearly forty-five minutes. He hoped it would give him time to get his head straight, but by the time he got there, he was on the verge of losing it.

"Corey! Dude, haven't seen you in a long time." He was surprised the bouncer at the door remembered him.

"Yeah. It's been over a year." A year since he started seeing Jack.

"Well, get the fuck in here man." He opened the door and let Corey in. He was happy that worked out because he hadn't wanted to pay the cover. This was the one place he knew he could get in, have a few drinks, and possibly leave with someone willing to give him what he needed. It'd been a regular hang out before meeting Jack.

He made his way through the crowd of jumping, grinding bodies, many of which were half naked, and found the bar. He squeezed himself in between a few bodies, but didn't bother looking at the bartender. All he had to do was wait. It all felt too familiar, even after all this time.

Jack would totally hate him being at this place. Why had he returned here? It felt like revisiting the scene of the crime. Could he find another Jack? Would Jack be here looking for his replacement? Probably not. Jack was too classy for the Dragon Club.

He felt the familiar constriction on his heart as if those metal barbs were still poking him. How was that possible when he didn't have a heart left?

"Hey, what you drinking?" Soft words purring in his ear interrupted his maudlin thoughts.

"Whatever you're buying me," Corey answered before he even turned to look at who had spoken. When he did turn, a tall, thin man in his mid-thirties stood beside him, practically pressed against his body. He had a long face with defined features. His dark blond hair was cut business short.

"Rum and Coke?"

"Sure." Corey licked at his lips and flashed him a smile. He could smile for a drink, especially when the guy buying was cute. He was no Jack. He lacked that sophistication and poise, but there was only one Jack anyway, and he'd shoved him away.

The guy buying him a drink leaned over the bar and flashed cash at the bartender. It didn't take long before they both had drinks in hand. "I'm Eric."

"Corey."

Eric gestured Corey to follow him to a less crowded area. The dance music was loud and pulsing. Lights flashed, red and green and blue. The place reeked of alcohol, sweat and sex. Eric wore jeans that he filled out nicely and a blue button up shirt with a dark tie with a knot that had been yanked down low. His loafers were black and probably Kenneth Cole or some other equally decent brand. They weren't cheap off-brand sneakers like Corey wore along with his dirty jeans and plain white t-shirt. Corey wished he'd taken at least some of the nice clothes Jack had bought for him.

"Haven't seen you here," Eric said loudly, leaning in to be heard over the music.

"Yeah. Been a while." Corey leaned in, too.

They sipped their drinks. Corey was nervous. Eric spent a lot of time just letting his eyes ease over Corey's body. Corey tried to ignore it, but found his eyes drawn back to Eric's. They were a hazel mix of intensity with gold and green flecks.

"Can I kiss you?" he asked.

Corey was surprised Eric had been so bold, but why not? Corey gave a nod and stood there letting Eric move in for the kiss. He had to lean down to meet Corey's mouth. The kiss was tentative at first, a brush of skin, and then a lick of his tongue across Corey's bottom lip. Corey opened his mouth, letting Eric's tongue dart in. It felt weird, surreal. Corey hadn't kissed anyone but Jack in over a year.

Eric broke the kiss and leaned in to Corey's chest. His mouth next to Corey's ear hissed out, "Nice."

Corey felt an arm snake around his waist and the heat of Eric's chest shoved against him. Corey wanted heat, skin, and more. He shifted his head until he was face to face with Eric, then closed the distance and pushed his lips against Eric's. Corey immersed himself in the intensity of Eric's kiss.

Eric bit down on Corey's bottom lip and pulled back, racking his teeth across skin making Corey's eyes flutter against his will. Eric nuzzled against his ear. "More?" Eric asked.

"Yes." Corey's answer came quickly.

Eric slid his hand underneath Corey's shirt. The tips of his fingers skimmed across Corey's stomach and up his chest until it found his left nipple, and the band aid there. Corey shoved his hand over to the other one and Eric pinched it hard. Corey hissed between his teeth.

"Sorry," Eric said.

Corey gave him a quirky smile and moved Eric's hand to his cock, so he could feel just how hard he was from that one pinch. "Like it," Corey said into Eric's ear. "More."

Eric smiled wide, showing straight white teeth. "All right," he mouthed, soundlessly. He nodded toward the back door of the club.

Corey's heart pounded loose without the barbs, thinking that his needs might just be met. His cock pulsed against the zipper of his jeans, as if agreeing with his heart.

They wouldn't go far from the club. He'd be safe enough. That thought was fleeting though and nothing else mattered when Eric gripped Corey's ass as they walked toward the exit.

Behind the club, a wide ally allowed for additional parking. Eric clicked his key fob and his car responded with a loud tone. Corey looked up at him.

"Don't worry, we're not going anywhere," Eric answered his unspoken question.

Eric's car was parked parallel along the wall of the adjacent brick building. There was just enough room to open the passenger side door and still be able to move around. It felt a little more secluded than just being in the open alley, making Corey feel a little more secure.

Sitting sideways in the seat with his legs outside of the car, Eric pulled Corey up between his thighs and unbuttoned his jeans. He pulled Corey's pants and underwear down around his knees in one good yank and started licking at Corey's cock. "Nice," he muttered, sliding his hands around Corey's waist.

Corey stared down into Eric's hazel eyes, hoping and praying for more, more than just a blow job, more pain to wrap around the pleasure. Maybe a little pain would mean he really didn't need Jack.

Eric's fingers swept down Corey's crack, sending tingles up his spine. He stood up and pushed Corey down toward the interior of the car. "Lean in, put your hands down."

Corey silently obeyed.

"What's your stops, Corey?"

Corey looked over his shoulder. Eric was fumbling with his pants with one hand and running his finger down Corey's crack with the other. Corey managed a shrug. "No pictures. Use a condom."

"Mm. You'll let me fuck you?"

"If you have a condom."

"Do you need lube? Open the glove box."

Corey reached up and popped the compartment open. A box of three extra sensitive condoms sat right on top. He reached in and pulled one out of the box, handing it back to Eric with a little shrug. "This is good. I'm ready," he said, happy he had done some prep before he'd left the apartment.

"It's still gonna hurt."

Corey didn't say anything. He watched as Eric rolled the condom over his long cock.

"You like that, don't you?"

"Fuck me, already." Corey wiggled his ass to get Eric's attention back. He wanted to feel the pain, feel the burn.

A moment later, Eric slammed into Corey from behind. Corey called out, bracing himself against the center console and pushed back, taking Eric in. He savored the pain. The burning sent his mind drifting to his zone like flipping on his own personal masochistic switch. For that moment he had peace.

"Don't you dare come, Corey. If you shoot on my seats I'll be pissed. Don't come until I say. Okay?"

"Yes, yes. Fuck me."

Eric pulled back slow and then thrust back in hard, before picking up a more steady, yet punishing rhythm. Corey pushed back, falling in sync with Eric's grinding hips. As Eric started losing his rhythm, Corey was getting close. Eric's cock thumped hard against Corey's prostate, making him call out,

"Jack."

"Fuck!" Eric came just that second, but Corey could tell he was pissed. He pulled out quick and tossed the used rubber against the wall. "Fuck you. When you're with me, you're fucking *with* me. Don't be calling out some other dude's name."

"Sorry. I'm sorry, Eric."

He leaned over and pulled Corey out of the car. He shoved him up against the brick wall and circled his throat with one thick hand. "I'll make you sorry," he said through clenched teeth. He was right in Corey's face, his hot breath exhaling over Corey's mouth.

Corey felt the first real tinge of fear. He couldn't breathe through Eric's tight grip on his throat. He was sure Eric could feel his heart racing, as he pushed his chest up against Corey's. The rough brick scraped across his bare ass.

Eric let go of his throat and shoved at his shoulders. "Turn around." Corey obeyed quickly, terrified to anger Eric again. He felt his feet being kicked out. "Spread 'em farther. Good boy," Eric said, as Cory submitted.

Without warning, he smacked Corey hard on the ass. Corey's cock jumped with the first smack and thickened painfully hard on the second. "Oh, you do like this."

Corey felt Eric's hand circling his cock. With each smack, Eric jacked Corey's dick. The pain and pleasure mingled erotically in Corey's head, pushing him along the edge of ecstasy and agony, right along the brink of orgasm. Eric's swats on his ass stung and the pulling on his cock felt like heaven.

Corey groaned. "Eric, please."

"Please, what?"

With his earlier fears momentarily lost in this drowning sensation, Corey blurted out, "Please, I have to come. Please, Eric."

"I'm glad you remember my name. Come then. Go ahead, I've got you." He smacked Corey's ass once more and jerked, making Corey shoot out his seed against the brick wall.

Eric laughed as Corey pulled his pants back up. He reached into Corey's pocket and took his phone. A moment later another cell was ringing. "Here. I'll call you." He handed Corey back his phone and circled around to the driver's side of his car. "This was fun, baby," he called out as he ducked into his car and cranked it up. Corey watched him drive away.

When Eric was out of site, Corey looked at his phone. His hands shook so hard, he almost dropped it. He saved the number Eric had called to his contacts and labeled it XXX. Then speed dialed Dirk. He wanted to take a shower desperately. He felt dirty and sore and couldn't see himself walking home.

Dirk picked up on the second ring. "Corey? What's up? You okay?"

"No. I want to come home." He had to fight back the tears. He was falling apart.

"It's okay. I'm coming to get you."

"I'm at the Dragon."

He waited in the alley squatting down by the brick wall, not wanting to even move until his phone rang. "Yeah," he answered.

"Where are you? I'm here."

"I'm coming."

He walked down the alley to the side street and around to the front of the club. When he got to the main street, he could see Dirk's Honda across the way, so he waved and crossed over to it. He didn't feel safe until he was sitting in the car with the seat belt on.

"What happened? You okay?" Dirk's voice was so full of concern that he had Corey choking back tears again.

"I don't want to talk about it."

Dirk put his hand on Corey's knee. "It's okay. It'll be okay."

"Thanks."

Once they were back at the apartment, Corey made a beeline for the shower. He had to get the smell of the club, Eric, and the dirty alley off of him. Afterward, sitting on the couch, he felt a lot calmer.

He was glad Dirk didn't push him to talk about it. His

bottom felt warm and well used, satiated, despite the fear and awkwardness of the situation. He was able to stretch out on the couch and quickly drift off to sleep.

17 Unraveled

Jack sat on his couch staring into his coffee cup and wondering if he was going to make it through another day. Corey had destroyed him. Things would never be the same. His throat tightened as tears threatened him for the millionth time since Corey had left. He knew he was wallowing in his misery, but actually doing anything else seemed too difficult. He didn't know how to fix his broken heart any more than he knew how to get Corey back.

His cell phone rang. It was his assistant, Ann. "What?" he answered.

"Good morning, Mr. Wolfe. You have a few appointments today, including one with Mr. Killebrew, the C.E.O. of Trident Security Services? He flew in especially for this meeting and they're the top firm supporting your venture."

"I know who they are, but I'm not up to this."

Ann sighed. "I know. I get it, but Mr. Wolfe—"

"Call me Jack. You're only pulling this *Mr. Wolfe* crap because you know I don't want to go in."

"Fine, Jack. Do yourself a favor and figure out how to get Corey back. He was good for you."

"If I knew how to do that, do you think I'd be sitting here feeling sorry for myself?"

Jack heard a roll of feminine laughter. "I never thought I'd ever see the likes of you sitting around feeling sorry for yourself. That's so not you, Jack. Figure out what to do. Do something—anything. You have to move forward one way or another. Call Mr. Moore. You know he'll help you. Just suck up that pride a little. Hm?"

"I know. I'm just not ready for Kenneth's crap yet. See if you can get Dwayne to handle Killebrew for me, will you?"

"Yes sir, I got it covered. Figure it out, okay. Bye, Jack."

Jack hung up and tossed the cell phone across the couch. He knew Ann was right. He had to do something. His life had been reduced to sitting around and re-reading old texts from Corey. In his heart, the man was still his. He listened to old voicemail, just to hear his voice. He couldn't sleep in his own bed, because it was empty and cold and he kept expecting Corey's warm body to be there. He knew on some level that Corey had gotten to him, to his heart. He was more to him than a sub or a boyfriend. He was everything and Jack needed him home, or his world would never be the same.

Kenneth. Jack wondered if he'd written him off because of past issues with Colin. He'd thought a lot about what he'd said and maybe he was right. Maybe he wasn't, but either way sitting around doing nothing was not helping anything either. He needed to get some kind of discipline back in his life. It had been a long time since he'd felt this chaotic. Jack never thought about those days. The few times memories tried to creep up, he shoved them down hard. Jack didn't need to doubt himself; there was no room in his life for anything but strict compliance to the rules he'd set for himself and those in his life.

Jack needed to fix this, so he flipped through the contacts on his phone. Kenneth answered right away. "Moore here."

"Kenneth? It's Jack Wolfe."

"Jack!" He sounded genuinely pleased to hear from him. "I was hoping you'd call."

"Why?"

"Hey. I can be concerned about you, Jack." His tone threw Jack off. He hadn't expected Kenneth to seem so involved.

"Okay," he sputtered in his confusion.

Kenneth rolled right over Jack's reaction and went straight into his explanation. "So, listen, I had a long talk with Colin. I assure you I dressed him down sufficiently and he understands now. He won't interfere with you and your sub."

"He's more than that."

"I know and that's fine. We get it. Colin gets it."

"That doesn't matter. We still aren't back together and that's why I'm calling."

"Oh. Sorry to hear that. How can I help?"

Jack stood up and started pacing his living room. He didn't even know what to ask. How to get Corey back? How to move on? How to deal with this depression? "I don't even know, Ken."

"I'm good at listening, Jack. Just tell me about it. Then, we can figure it out." His voice was calming, soothing. This was why he was Jack's Dom of Doms. He didn't make Jack feel less of a Dom himself by sharing what was going on.

"So, I'm losing it. I can't think about anything else. I haven't been in to work and I don't want to even get out of bed most mornings. I...I...I'm a tangled mess. Oh God! I really am losing it."

"Jack. Take a deep breath."

Jack sat on the floor, leaning back against the couch and took a few deep breaths. "Thank you," he muttered when he felt more in control.

"You really need to get this out and I think Corey needs to hear it. He needs to know what you're going through without him."

"Maybe. But—"

"No, Jack. Don't hem and haw. He needs to know just how much you care. You keep saying he's more than a sub, but have you told him that? Have you shown him that?"

"No, and right now, he won't let me."

"Won't let you?"

"Yeah, he won't answer my calls or texts. I'm afraid to go over there. To where he's staying. He'd probably slam the door in my face."

"No."

Jack chuckled without humor.

"Okay, Jack. How about this. Write him a letter. Be sincere. Maybe he'll read that and you'll break through to him."

"I don't know, Ken. I'm not good at that kind of shit."

"Maybe that's okay. It only matters that you're trying. Don't just give up on him. I'm betting he needs to hear this from you, even if he doesn't know it or want to admit it."

Jack grumbled under his breath. He knew Kenneth was probably right, but it wasn't going to be easy at all. "Yeah? Maybe."

"Okay. Seriously, Jack. Come back to the group. It would help you. There's a meeting next week."

"Colin's still there?"

Jack could hear the long sigh before Kenneth answered. "Don't hang yourself up on him. He's just not that important. Unless you make him that important."

Jack wanted to ask him what was important then. He didn't want to see Colin. Maybe he didn't want to see any of them. Watching them with their subs while he was alone did not sound like a supportive evening. "I'll think about it."

"Fine. Call me anytime, Jack."

"Thanks." Jack hung up, not sure how much he would actually think about it. He had more important things on his mind and maybe Kenneth was right about putting his feelings down on paper.

Jack fired up his laptop and opened his email. If Corey wasn't ready to listen, maybe he would read it. He typed his heart out:

Corey - baby!

I know you don't want to talk, but please read this. I love you so much and my life is empty without you. I'm miserable and making everyone else around me miserable, too!

You are my world. All I ever wanted to do was love and protect you. Failing you was the worst mistake I've ever made. Please come home and work this out. We can figure it out together, just like everything else. I don't have to be your Dom to love you, Corey. We can work without that, if need be. I miss you, not our sessions. I miss seeing you at the breakfast table every morning. I miss your stuff all over the sink in the bathroom. I miss hearing your heartbeat next to mine as we lay down at the end of every day. I miss waking up to your cold feet tangled up with mine. I miss your voice, your smile, your enticing green eyes, and I miss everything about you. We're better together. Please, please come home.

I love you,
Jack

He read the letter over three times and hit send.

18 Tumult

Corey woke up some time in the afternoon. His roommates were still out, and Corey hardly knew what to do with the day. He checked his phone and saw five missed calls, so he dialed his voicemail.

Call number one was Eric, which left Corey a bit confused: *"Last night was fun baby, I'd like to see you again. Give me a call back."*

Corey deleted the call, wondering what he was doing thinking about Eric.

The second call was more surprising: *"Corey, Corey Roman? This is Ann, Jack's assistant. I hope you remember me. Look, if there's anything I can do to help you two get back together, let me know. Okay? Even if you just want to talk about it. Call me."*

Corey deleted that call as well, sure Jack had put her up to calling. He remembered Ann as being very assertive and one of the few people who got away with bossing Jack around. He liked her, but he certainly wasn't returning her call.

The next call was Eric again: *"What's going on? Not answering your phone? Call back already."*

Eric's voice sounded frustrated, and his third message came right on the heels of his second: *"If you don't call me soon, the next time we meet, you'll get more than just a little spanking."*

Corey wasn't sure what to think. He sounded irritated and playful at the same time. It scared him a little and he thought seriously of changing his number.

The final voicemail was from Jillian. *"Hey, Corey. Listen. I haven't heard from your interview yet, that's not why I'm calling. I have a friend who's a journalist and she'd really love to interview Jack. His project is up for a big award and she's trying to get all the candidates, only his assistant won't put her through. I thought, you know, since I'm helping you. Well, see if Jack will do it, please?"*

Corey felt guilty. He wanted to help Jillian, but could he really call Jack?

He fired up his laptop and clicked on the email. Maybe he'd get more info from Jillian first. He had a bunch of spam that he deleted, then he saw Jack's message. He opened the email and read it slowly. He read it again.

He still wanted Corey.

Maybe it was time to stop messing around. Getting his fix from other places wasn't working and he loved Jack, insanely and without reason. How could he just pick up the phone and ask to go home after he'd pretty much told Jack to fuck off?

Maybe he could use Jillian's friend as an excuse to break the ice. He dialed Jack's number and he answered on the second ring. "Corey?"

"Yeah. Hi, Jack. Uh, listen. Jillian's been helping me look for work, and uh, she wanted to see if I'd get you to do an interview with her friend."

"What?"

"It's no big deal."

"Are you kidding me? You want a fucking favor? I can't even believe you. After all this?"

Corey started stuttering, "No, not really, Jack listen..." but Jack didn't listen. He yelled a few choice curse words and hung up.

Tears fell unrestrained down Corey's cheeks. Had he lied? Did he not really want Corey? Had Corey really pushed him too far? The confusion and pain took him right back to that first night when they split up. He never felt so alone. Corey buried his head in the pillow and sobbed, dropping his phone to the floor. He'd ruined everything.

He heard the front door open, but he couldn't stop his crying, as much as he wanted to.

"Corey?" Stan came in and knelt down next to the couch. "Dude, are you okay?"

"God, no. I can't take this anymore," Corey breathed out between his sobs.

"Look. I can't say I understand what you're going through and I barely know you, but I'm here and if you're cool with Dirk, you're cool with me. You know?"

Corey sat up and wiped at his eyes. "I'm sorry. I...I thought Jack wanted me back and I called him, and he was a dick. I'm stupid for thinking. For hoping."

Stan slid beside him on the couch and put his arm around his shoulder. "Look. You know? You're right. Maybe you need to just move on or something?"

Corey could tell Stan was trying to be a friend, comforting, but he couldn't think straight. He wanted something to ease his burning heart. He wanted the sting of a single tail across his back. "Shit. Where's my phone?"

Stan handed the cell to Corey, picking it up off of the floor. He let his fingers dance over the pad, sending Eric a text: *Just got up. Sorry. Want to play?*

"I really gotta get out of here. I'm fucking losing it."

"Do you want a ride somewhere or something?"

Corey shrugged. "Maybe. I don't know."

His phone beeped with a text back from Eric: *Meet me in front of the club - one hour. Don't be late.*

"Uh, no. But thanks. I got it. See ya later." He bolted out the front door. He couldn't deal with Stan being nice to him and looking at him with pity in his eyes. He knew how to take care of his bleeding heart. Eric would take care of it. He hadn't really hurt Corey the night before and he was willing to play a little, even if he seemed like he didn't know what he was doing. Corey could teach him. Eric was no Jack, but it was better than sitting around crying for someone he could never get back.

Corey stood in front of the club forty minutes later, breathing hard from his fast walk. He wasn't about to be late.

He wished he'd had time to shower, shave, and prep, but it couldn't be helped since Eric hadn't given him much time. His face had two days of growth now, and he hoped it'd make him look rugged, rather than unkempt. Jack had always like him clean shaven. It didn't matter what the hell Jack wanted anymore.

He watched for Eric's car, not sure he remembered what the man had driven or what color it was, but he knew it had brown vinyl seats and a sturdy center console. He smiled remembering Eric fucking him across the passenger seat. That hadn't been bad at all. Hard, burning, painful, and so good. He wanted that kind of release again, so desperately, that he ignored that knot in his stomach. He needed someone's attention, even if that was Eric.

A dark red Chevy Impala pulled to the curb and the window rolled down. "Hey, sugar. Get in!" Eric called from the driver's side.

Corey opened the door and sat in the passenger's seat. "Hey, Eric."

"Hey, yourself." He leaned in and kissed Corey quickly on the lips. "I got a hotel room. Okay with you?"

"Yeah, sure." Corey's heart thumped, ready to get going and get on with it.

Eric pulled away from the curb and drove smoothly in and out of traffic, driving to an even seedier part of town. He pulled into the parking lot of a rundown hotel. "It's cheap, but they're clean. I've been here before," he said, reassuringly, but Corey felt anything but reassured.

Corey followed him into the room. It smelled like bleach. There were two queen sized beds side by side and an old television against the wall sitting on top of the one pressed-board dresser in the room. The carpeting looked so thin, he could swear he saw the cement underneath through the weave. There were no pictures on the walls and the only lighting in the main room was the orangish glow from the one lamp jutting out between the beds. The front curtains were pulled shut. On the far side of the beds, a double sink with a florescent light glaring down marked the start of the bathroom area. To the right was a door that hid the tub and toilet. It was about as bare bones as a hotel could get.

"Get comfortable," Eric grumbled as he pulled off his tie and dress slacks, and started unbuttoning his shirt.

Corey silently followed, kicking off shoes, dropping his jeans, and tossing them over the bed against the far wall. His t-shirt followed. He stood between the beds wearing just a plain pair of white briefs. It reminded him of his early days in college, finally out of his parent's house and able to explore. He went through a lot of guys back then. None of them were too interested in more than a quick fuck, which was okay, but Corey had always wanted more. Jack wasn't his first, but he'd been the first to make Corey feel that he was worth more than a hookup. Corey wondered if that had ever really been true. Sometimes Jack made him feel more like a possession, telling him what to do and how to do it, in and out of the bedroom. He felt like a kept man, something to be cherished, but not an equal part of a relationship. At other times, it seemed like Jack wanted him like no other, that he was trying for more. So, what was that worth to him? Was that what Corey wanted?

Eric stepped over and wrapped his hand behind Corey's neck, pulling him closer. He attacked Corey's mouth with lips and tongue. He rubbed the back of his hand against the scruff along Corey's jaw. Releasing Corey from the kiss, he shoved him down on the bed nearest the window. "You give head, Corey? Want to suck me off? Then, I'll see if I can give you some of what you need."

Corey had no illusions that this was anything but a hookup. The energy spent kissing was cold, but he still said, "Sure."

Eric pulled his briefs down to his thighs, letting his cock pop out. Corey leaned in and licked at it, then took it between his lips.

"Ugh! I want to fuck your mouth, Corey. Get on your knees."

Corey obeyed. Even though Eric was no Dom, he was

certainly an aggressive Alpha-type. It was enough for Corey to respond submissively, and he opened his mouth to let Eric shove his cock in. He pushed in to the back of Corey's throat, grabbing Corey's head and pumping in and out of his mouth feverishly until he was squirting, hot down Corey's throat. He pulled out before he was finished, and squirted across Corey's chin, neck, and chest.

"Damn, sorry about that." He didn't sound sorry. Corey wiped at it with the back of his hand. "Let me get you a towel," Eric finally offered.

After he cleaned up. Eric nodded to the bed again. "So, uh, you like the bondage stuff, right?"

Corey nodded. He wasn't sure he wanted to let Eric tie him up. He was nowhere near secure enough. He wasn't sure he wanted to do anything else with Eric. He was falling apart.

"So, my boyfriend wants me to use a flogger on him."

"You have a boyfriend?"

"I've never used one before. I thought maybe I can test it on you and get the hang of it. Cool?"

Corey rolled his eyes. He wanted to leave, but maybe he could help Eric out and get some of his itch scratched at the same time. "Okay, I can help you. But, if I say red, you have to stop. That's the safe word. Got it?"

"Over the bed?"

Corey sighed and lay on his stomach across the bed. Eric came behind him and pulled his briefs down to his thighs. "I want to smack your ass and your back, okay?"

"Sure." Corey crossed his arms under his chest.

"Can I tie your wrists instead?"

Corey rolled on his side and stared at Eric. Was he really so clueless. "With what?"

"My tie?" He picked the blue and black material off the floor and held it out to Corey.

"Fine." Corey held his wrists together and let Eric casually knot them together. He pulled at the makeshift restraint. He could get out of it easy enough, but it held. "Okay." He rolled back on his stomach with his arms stretched out over his head and bound with Eric's tie.

"You're sure a sexy thing, like that."

"Thank you."

Corey felt the soft leather of the flogger slide down his shoulders and back, teasing softly down his spine and across his ass. He started striking a little harder, but not hard enough.

"Flick your wrist more," Corey directed.

Eric snapped the flogger across Corey's ass. "Like that?"

"Better."

"Okay. I'm getting the hang of it now." He snapped the flogger up and down his back and ass, getting better with each progression.

"Better. You can go harder," Corey told him, wanting to feel the heat of it.

He wondered if this would be how his life would go now without Jack: going to cheap hotel rooms for hookups with novices wanting to learn how to flog their boyfriends. He needed a good Dom, if he couldn't have Jack. He wondered why he hadn't asked Jillian for help with that and vowed to do that once Eric was finished with *Dom Your Boyfriend 101*.

Eric started laying into Corey's back with a decent rhythm. He felt the stinging burn and started to float, concentrating on the bite of each lash as the rest of the world faded to a black distance that he no longer had to look at.

Too soon, Eric tired of it. "Your ass is really red. Can I fuck you?"

"Mm-hm. Use a condom."

Eric pulled at Corey's hips, lifting him up off the bed. He felt cool lube and the plastic-like sheath of the condom pushing against his ass, and he pushed back into Eric's cock. It filled him hard. Corey cried out a little, but he was still floating from the flogging. The extra pain only sent him higher, racing through him like a can of Coke first thing in the morning, scorchingly refreshing against a rough throat. His body wanted to lift off the bed, as his heartbeat slowed and his head slipped further into that static-filled white noise of oblivion.

Corey could feel his balls pulling up tight, his body

becoming hypersensitive and ready to come. He needed that release, chased after it. Before Corey could get close enough to the edge, Eric was pulling out. "Damn, you're so tight, so hot."

Corey moaned and bucked into the hotel bed, his cock touchy and wanting to come. He needed more of everything, friction, pain, and mostly, he wanted to keep flying.

"I've never known such a pain-slut," Eric said. "You want to come, Corey?"

"Y...Yes." He fought against the pull of earth.

Eric leaned over his back. Corey could feel the cool sweat of Eric's chest sliding down his back. Something scratched at his side, and a sharp stabbing pain in his back, just under his ribs made him jump up off the bed. He screamed, "Eric! What the fuck? Red! Stop!" His head immediately started pounding as he was ripped away from subspace.

"Just want to see how far you'll let me push you."

Corey felt wet across his back and suspected he was bleeding. He turned to check it out and Eric jumped him, pushing his shoulders and back against the headboard. He gripped Corey's throat, holding him tight. Corey could feel his fingers digging in where the bruises still were that he'd left from their night in the club parking lot.

"Get off me," Corey choked out.

Eric was breathing in his face. "You know you like this."

Corey shoved at him. His head felt tingly. "Off," he grunted. He could barely catch a breath.

Eric leaned away and backhanded Corey, smacking his eye and cheek, and sending him flying to the floor between the beds. "Get the fuck out of here, pain-whore."

Corey yanked his hands out of Eric's stupid tie, glad he didn't let the idiot cinch it tight and grabbed his jeans off the bed, shoving his legs in them. He grabbed his t-shirt and headed to the door, pulling his jeans over his ass as he went. His head was spinning. Sweat dripped from his forehead and the back of his neck, and his side was dripping, too, with sticky blood that quickly darkened the edge of his waistband.

Eric grabbed his arm, digging fingernails into his bicep.

"You know you want this. Call me for more, bitch."

Corey jerked out of his grip. "Fuck you."

He was out the door. He reached down inside his jeans, pulling up his briefs and buttoning his fly. The parking lot lurched out beneath his bare feet. He dug in his pocket for his phone as he stumbled down to the main drag. He was dizzy, wet; still bleeding? Confused, he tapped his phone, dialing from the contacts.

A cab was driving toward him and he raised his arm to flag it down.

"Corey?" the baritone timber of Jack's voice answered. He would know the voice anywhere.

"I'm so sorry. I'm sorry. I need you, Jack. I..."

"Where are you Corey? Are you okay?"

His jeans were cloying, wet on the right side. "No. I don't know. Wait."

The cab pulled over. "Need a ride kid?"

Corey practically fell into the back seat. "Yeah," he grunted, holding phone out toward the cabby and closed his eyes. The world was spinning and he was so cold.

19 Redemption

"Corey? Corey?" Jack shouted in the phone.

"He passed out. He's bleeding," a strange voice said into the phone.

"What? Who is this?" Panic crawled up Jack's spine and twisted in his gut.

"Just a cabbie. I'm taking your boy to the hospital."

Jack pulled at his bangs. "Which one?"

"Mount Sinai."

"I'll pay you for the ride plus your time and tip, if you stick around, okay?" It was certainly the least he could do. What happened to Corey? Bleeding? The guy said Corey was bleeding. Where was he? What had happened? This guy didn't know. Jack's throat constricted, feeling too tight to breathe.

"Sure. Just don't want him bleeding to death in my back seat."

Bleeding! Oh God! "Okay. Drive. Go!" Jack's world spun out of control.

He wiped his sweaty hands on his shirt before reluctantly disconnecting the line. What else could he do? He speed dialed Ann. "It's Jack. Corey's been taken to Mount Sinai. Something's wrong. I'm going there now."

He called Mick on his way down. The limo was ready when he got to the garage. "Mick. You will not be fired for breaking the speed limit." Corey was bleeding? Unconscious?

What the hell? His heart couldn't decide if it wanted to play wall-ball against his ribs or jump up into his throat, making him swallow hard.

"That's a good thing. Am I going to get fired for hanging out with you at the hospital? 'Cause I'm doing that, too."

"No."

A few minutes later, Jack's phone rang. He didn't recognize the number, but given the situation, he answered it anyway. "Jack Wolfe."

"Uh, yeah. Sorry to disturb you, Mr. Wolfe. This is Dirk. Uh, have you heard from Corey? I'm kinda worried. I hate calling you, but..."

"But, what? Spit it out."

"Well, my roommate, Stan, saw him a few hours ago and he was very upset and he just took off and now he's not answering his phone."

What he didn't say was that Corey had been upset about Jack. Corey had finally reached out, and Jack ripped him a new one. What the hell was wrong with him? Just because it hadn't happened the way Jack wanted, he turned his back? *I'm just an asshole.*

"...and, Stan said he had some nasty bruising around his neck. I hadn't noticed when I'd picked him up from the club last night, but I think someone was playing rough with him. And you know Corey is, uh, you know?"

Jack knew better than anyone how Corey was. He wiped his tears with the back of his hand. This had to be his fault. All of it. "Mount Sinai hospital. I'm on my way now."

"Fuck."

"Yeah. Guess I'll see you there?"

"Yes, sir."

The phone went dead. If Dirk was calling Jack for information, it was bad. "Damn it." Corey what did you do?

He wanted to climb out of the limo and fly to the hospital. He desperately needed to see Corey alive and well. Thoughts of a beaten, bruised, bloodied Corey raced through his head. Sorrow threatened to drown him one second, then blind rage welled up over him the next. He rolled down the window and let the wind blow in his face, hoping to just keep his insides together until they made it to the hospital and could determine the situation.

Memories threatened to overtake him. From so long ago, when he'd been a boy and could do nothing to help his family or himself. He'd had to do what the adults said with no say in his own situation. He listened and obeyed foster parents and teachers, biting his tongue and biding his time. Even as young as twelve, Jack knew there would come a day when he would have the power to control his own destiny. He'd make it happen through sheer will. Yet, this time it was different. It was back to being twelve and being jerked around from home to home with no choice, because he couldn't control the doctors and hospital staff or the cabbie that could have left Corey on the side of the road to die.

Jack bit back those memories, refusing to let them out, refusing to let them take control of him.

He shifted in his seat, unable to settle. He flicked through the contacts and tapped Kenneth's number before he even realized he should stop himself. He'd never asked for help, but maybe this one time? With Corey hurt, he could forgive himself almost anything.

"Jack! Hey! I didn't think I'd be hearing from you so soon," he answered.

"Kenneth. Uh. It's Corey. He's been hurt and I don't know what to do..."

"Hey, hey. We'll figure it out." His voice was soft and reassuring, but Jack wasn't a sub and he needed something more than that.

"We're on the way to the Mount Sinai." His words hung in the air. Just a statement. Yet, Jack was asking for more from Kenneth than he'd ever asked from anyone and he didn't know how to voice it.

"Okay. I get it. I'll be there. Okay?"

"Yes. Please."

Jack didn't know what Kenneth picked up on from just

his voice, but he'd been a Dom for a long time, so it shouldn't have surprised him. "Jack. Take a deep breath," he commanded in a tone that wouldn't allow Jack to disobey.

He breathed in hard. "Yes."

"Exhale."

Jack blew it out slowly. "Yes."

"Good. I'll be there, but you need to keep your shit together. For Corey. Okay?"

"Yes." There was nothing else to say. Kenneth was right and hearing Kenneth's authoritative voice, Jack knew he could do it. For Corey.

Hours later Jack was finally allowed in to see Corey since he had no other family near. He was unconscious. They'd stitched him up, but he'd lost a lot of blood. He had a puncture wound to his kidney. The doctor's said he'd be all right, but Jack didn't know about that. He would live, but *all right* might never happen, judging by the bruises on his neck and face. Jack wanted to kill whoever did this to him. Every jealous and possessive tendency he ever had was choking him as he stared down at his ex-lover, his Corey.

"Baby, I love you. What did you do? Hm?" He held Corey's hand and watched his eyelids twitch. He wouldn't be waking up for a while, but Jack wanted to offer him what comfort he could give.

Mick was waiting outside with Dirk and the new roommate, Stan. Jack had paid the cabbie twice the fair. Then he got a good look at the back seat covered with Corey's blood and gave him an extra fifty to get it cleaned. Ann had come and left. She promised to call Jillian in the morning, and he knew she would fill Kenneth in on Corey's status.

He ran his hands through his hair, nervously. The trauma doctor said he'd been in shock and they gave him blood and stitched him up. They ran blood tests and x-rays afterwards to rule out any other injuries. They also pumped him full of antibiotics. Now, he just needed to rest. Once they were happy he had no infections, they'd send him home. Maybe tomorrow or the day after. Home where? With Jack? With Dirk?

Jack wondered if he should call Corey's parents, but decided to hold off a little longer. Having them storm the ER probably wouldn't be a good idea, since Corey's parents were a little on the crazy side, and they'd probably do all they could to run Jack off, if they even bothered to show up at all.

No. He wouldn't bring them in unless he had to. Corey wouldn't want them there, anyway. He didn't get along well with them. Jack wanted to lecture him that he should try harder with his parents since he was lucky he had parents. Jack had lost his so long ago, before he'd ever had a chance to really know them. But then again, if they'd still been around, there was no guarantee Jack would get along with them. In fact, given what little he knew about them, he probably wouldn't. He snorted, and shoved the old memory aside. He didn't want to think about them. Not now. Not ever.

His thumb rubbed over the back of Corey's fingers. Corey's eyes fluttered. "Jack?"

"I'm here, baby." He leaned in close, brushing his lips softly across Corey's cheek.

His eyes scanned the room, seemingly out of focus. "Where am I?"

"Hospital. You were bleeding. Do you remember what happened?"

"No. Where were you?" His voice was confused, gentle.

Jack thought his heart would break. "I was waiting for you, baby."

"M'Kay." He closed his eyes.

"Get some rest, baby."

He went back to sleep. Soon a nurse came in and asked him to leave. Her thin blond hair was pinned back and she wore Hello Kitty scrubs. Jack liked her tender manner.

"He woke up a little," he told her.

She started checking all the beeping machines. "Good.

You need to go get some rest. Maybe some food. Then, come back. He'll want you here when he really wakes up. Maybe a couple of hours, seriously."

"Okay."

Jack walked down the hall. Three male heads jerked up when he came into the waiting room. "He will most likely sleep a few more hours. He's going to be fine, though," he said before they started in on whether he was really okay. He sank into one of the chairs; thankfully it had thick cushions. He rubbed his hands over his face.

Mick sat beside him. "I've got the limo parked out front. Why don't you go crash in the back for a while, boss? If they come out, I'll call you."

Jack shook his head. "Nah. I'll just sit here and wait."

"Okay."

"Why don't you offer that to the boys?" He nodded to Dirk and Stan who were sitting across the room, slumped down in their own chairs.

"Sure." Mick stood up.

"Mick?"

"Yes, sir?"

"You've got a big raise coming, son." He leaned back and shut his eyes, not listening to any thank you the man might be tempted to offer. Jack didn't want thanked. He took care of those that had his back. Always.

Jack had no idea how long he'd been scrunched up in his chair, but he was startled when a gruff voice called his name. Jack stood up to see a man wearing slacks, a rumpled shirt, and a leather jacket staring at him. He held his hand out. "I'm Detective Bishop."

Jack shook his hand. "Jack Wolfe."

"The hospital reported the attack on Corey Roman. I need to ask you few questions about it."

"Sure. Of course, but I don't know how much help I'll be."

The detective nodded toward the chairs, and Jack sat back down. The detective sat on the edge of the seat next to him. "Well," he said, "I've interviewed the cabbie. He said Corey called you when it happened and you paid for the ride and more, plus you're the responsible party on his hospital bills."

"And?"

"I'm assuming you're partners? So, maybe you know who he was with or what he was doing?"

Jack shook his head. "I hadn't heard from him in a while...weeks." Jack nodded to Dirk who was slouched over a chair sideways, attempting some kind of rest. His jacket was over his head. "That's Dirk, his roommate. He'd know more."

Bishop pulled out a small note pad from his back pocket and jotted something down in it. A crease between his eyebrows dipped as he thought. "I need his cell phone."

"Sure." Jack pulled it out of his pocket and handed it to the detective.

"You're not officially a suspect or even a person of interest, but until he tells me otherwise." Bishop jabbed his pencil in the air. "Can't rule you out, either."

"Good."

"Good? Why?"

Jack crossed his arms and kicked his chin up a little. "That means you're doing a thorough investigation. I want the bastard that did this caught. I can't stand that someone hurt my Corey."

Bishop gave Jack an intense look and chewed the inside of his mouth. "Yeah. I also know that you were locked up not long ago for assault. Charges dropped."

"And?"

"You beat up your *boyfriend*?" He emphasized the word, but Jack wasn't sure if it was because he didn't approve of gay relationships, or if he doubted Corey was really his boyfriend. Maybe it just was Jack's own doubts.

Jack chuffed. "I beat up the asshole that thought he could

put his hands on my boyfriend."

The Detective gestured across the room. "Going to talk to this guy. Dirk, you said?"

Jack nodded and watched the detective cross to where Dirk was slumped down. He meant what he said. He didn't mind a little scrutiny, if it caught the attacker. Jack knew it would be much better for the police to catch him, because if Jack got there first, he'd likely kill the fucker.

Dirk answered the detective's questions with animation and hands waiving in the air. A few times, Dirk looked over at Jack and glanced away. He knew Dirk was telling the detective about his relationship with Corey, but he didn't know how much Dirk was spilling.

Resigned, Jack closed his eyes and leaned back in the chair. He couldn't control what Dirk said. He only hoped that the extent of how he played with Corey wouldn't come out for Corey's sake. He didn't know how much Corey had shared with his friends. He suspected what they knew was just the tip of the old proverbial iceberg. He doubted Corey went into depths about his masochism and fetishes. All Dirk probably knew was that the relationship was odd and Corey came home with bruises and a sore ass sometimes.

He drug his hand down his face. That was probably worse than the full explanation. It painted a picture of an abusive relationship, which was so far, far from the truth.

After a few minutes Detective Bishop stopped again by his chair. "I'm probably going to have some follow-up questions for you. Can I find you here later?"

"Yes. That's fine. I'll be here until they let Corey come home."

"Yeah." The detective chewed on the word. "I'll need to talk to him, too. When he wakes up."

"Of course. Detective." He offered the guy his hand again.

The detective shook it. Firm. Confident. Yet, his eyes questioned everything.

Jack sat in the uncomfortable chair with his head in his hands wondering how long it would be until he could see Corey again. His injuries really put their entire relationship into much better perspective for him. He knew he'd been a jerk, but even beyond that, Corey had been right; Jack had treated him like a possession.

He was really disgusted with all of his own dramatics over it, too. Jack had always been the guy to take action. His aunt had left him a small trust fund, hardly worth a damned thing, and Jack molded his investment into the company he owned today with real estate projects all over town. He'd grown his business into a multi-billion dollar success because he took what was his and took care of what was his. Unlike his parents.

"Jack?" A warm hand settled on his shoulder.

"Hey. Kenneth. Thanks for coming." He nodded to the uncomfortable seat next to him and Kenneth sat down, resting his hand on Jack's shoulder.

"You okay?"

"No." Jack shook his head and cleared his throat. "I'm not going to be okay until Corey is home and healthy."

"I get that. I'd be climbing the walls if it were Jillian in there." He leaned in closer and lowered his voice. "When something is wrong with our subs, it makes us Doms a bit on the crazy side."

Jack laughed. "A bit? Hell! Just for the record, I think we're already on the crazy side. We have to be to be...doing this."

"The lifestyle?"

"Um, yeah." Jack hadn't thought about his reasons for going down this path in some time. No, he thought he had everything under control, when really, he hadn't had anything under control.

"Nah. I think it's just another way of doing things. More intense than the vanilla-world. That's all."

"I don't know about that. I'm a pretty fucked up mess, Kenneth. I'm controlling and demanding—"

"Duh, Jack. You're a Dom," he interrupted.

"Not a very good one."

"Who's to judge? Hey. Let's take a walk." He nodded to the front doors, and Jack stood up. If the conversation got any deeper, he didn't really want anyone else around to hear it.

He followed Kenneth through the automatic doors and down the sidewalk toward the parking lot where Kenneth looked around. Sure that no others were close enough to overhear, he finally spoke up. "So, really, I think your biggest problem, Jack, is that you isolated yourself. All wrapped up in your new boy toy. You forgot that you need support. You need understanding. You need others from the community to help you focus on Corey."

"I'm not sure. What do you mean?" Jack had been questioning himself before, but Kenneth's words had him thinking he'd really done everything wrong. Every. Fucking. Single. Thing.

"You have to have your needs, emotional needs, met before you can give Corey what he needs. Your relationship should be ninety percent taking care of your sub. The other ten percent is enjoying his gift. If you aren't doing it like that." He shook his head. "I'm guessing something is off in your power balance if he left you. Like that." *Yeah, like that.*

"Fuck me sideways."

"Been there done that," Kenneth snickered.

Jack bumped his shoulder into Kenneth's. "Shut up."

"Jack. Don't let Colin keep you away from the group. But, if you can't get over it. Join a different group."

"Right," Jack nodded and clapped his hand on Kenneth's shoulder. "I get it. You're right on so many things. I don't think I would have even listened to you or anyone else if Corey hadn't..." The tears caught up in his throat. He couldn't finish the sentence.

"Okay. Call me. Keep me posted on how he is."

With a handshake, Kenneth left, but his words

reverberated around Jack's head for a long time. Why had he submitted to Colin all those years ago and why had he taken Corey on? To keep his life under control. That answer really was too simple, but maybe it was time for Jack to dig under the surface. Maybe it was time for him to pull those memories out and look at them. Even though it was the last thing he wanted to do, maybe for Corey, he didn't have a choice.

"Jack? Jack Wolfe?" This time it was a young woman in plain blue scrubs. Her hair was pulled back in a long brown pony tail. She wore just a splattering of makeup that made the gold flecks in her hazel eyes sparkle.

Jack stood up. "Yes, I'm Jack Wolfe."

"Can you please come help us with Corey? Now?" She turned, rushing away without waiting for his answer.

He followed quickly down the greenish hallway with its faded paint and scuffed linoleum floors. He was happy his long legs gave him a fast stride, as he barely caught up to her before she got to Corey's room. She pushed open the door, and he heard the problem immediately. Corey was crying and calling out for him.

Rushing to the bed, he cooed softly, "Corey, baby. It's okay. I'm here. I'm here." Corey was turned over on his injured side, fighting the nurses off and squirming all over the place. Jack wrapped his arm around his shoulder and ran the other hand through his sweat dampened hair. "Baby, baby. Calm down. It's Jack. Settle, baby settle."

"Jack?" Corey's voice was riddled with utter anguish.

"Relax, Corey." He used his Dom-voice tones to try and reach him through his panic. Corey blew out a long breath and his eyes cracked open. Jack made sure his face was down where Corey could see him. "It's okay, baby."

The nurse came up next to him. "We need to take the catheter out. Can you get him on his back? And, uh...can you please stay here while we do it?" Her voice sounded unsure and more than a little desperate. Normally, they'd send everyone out of the room for something like that, but he could tell Corey wasn't going to let them do anything without coaxing, and the nurse was smart enough to realize that was Jack's job.

"Yes, of course. Corey. The nurse is here to help. Turn on your back, baby."

Corey obeyed. His eyes didn't leave Jack's face. "Jack?" He grasped at Jack's arm.

"I know you're scared, baby. But, I'm here and no one is going to hurt you. The nurse has to take the catheter out. Okay? Can you let her?"

Corey nodded, blinking slowly, his gorgeous, thick black eyelashes brushing his cheek. "Yes."

The nurse took care of the issue, gave Corey another dose of pain killer in his IV and then turned to Jack. "The doctor will be in to talk to you in a few minutes. Thank you." She patted his arm before she turned away. Jack saw the relief and concern in her face.

Jack nodded. When she left, Corey finally relaxed into the bed. He closed his eyes and swallowed hard. "Are you okay?" He pushed Corey's curly bangs out of his eyes. His hair picked up deep burgundy highlights under the harsh florescent lighting.

"Yes. I guess." His voice was small, weak.

"Do you remember what happened?"

Corey nodded. "I don't want to talk about it."

"Okay, but you should know the hospital had to report your injury, and there's a detective that wants to talk to you."

Corey bit his lower lip and nodded. Eyes still closed.

"What is it, baby? What happened, hm?" He pet Corey's hair, and felt the tingling flutters in his heart and stomach when Corey leaned into his touch.

"I'm so sorry. I screwed up so bad. I'm sorry." Tears squeezed out of the corners of his eyes as he scrunched them tight.

"Corey. Oh, baby. This is not your fault. Whoever did this to you, they had no right." Jack's words were clogging in his throat. "None of this is your fault." He wiped at Corey's tears with his thumb.

"I...I tried. Jack, I tried. I stuck a fucking needle in my nipple. It wasn't enough." He started sobbing, turning his face into Jack's upper arm.

"What are you talking about?" Jack's stomach tightened and twisted. He was terrified of what Corey might say. Just how bad was it? "What did you do?"

"I stuck a sewing needle, here." He pointed to his chest. "I needed to feel it. To feel something."

"Oh, baby. Why couldn't you just call me?"

He started crying again. "I couldn't. I didn't know what to do. I just hurt so much. I wanted it to stop."

Jack pulled Corey up toward him, cradling as best he could over the side of the bed railing. "Corey. No matter what, I promise I'll be here for you."

"I don't know what that's like, Jack. I can't believe you. I've never had that. Never. Then, you did it to. Just like my parents."

"What do your parents have to do with this, baby?" Jack asked, softly, gently coaxing the information he needed from him.

"I called her. While I was at Dirk's. She always ignores me."

"Baby, I promise. I will not ignore you."

"But you did. You have. You've left me alone too many times. I can't trust you anymore."

Jack thought back to the most recent times. When he left him at the party and Colin Fucking Hayward violated him, but even before that. He'd left Corey alone and bound in the middle of a scene because his own head was fucked up. Corey was right. "I know, baby. I've fucked up a lot. But, I...I'm just human. I promise. If we move forward, I won't leave you alone again. Please? Give me a chance."

Corey sobbed again. "Jack!" He tightened his hold around

him, hoping to comfort him, but needing comfort himself.

"Corey, please come back. Please. Please come home with me." His own tears spilled out, hot down his cheek. He kissed the top of Corey's head. "I need you to be home." He needed to be sure Corey was safe.

"I want to go home," he sobbed. His tears tore at Jack's heart, unraveling him. Jack held him and let him cry.

When he finally settled down, he pulled away from Jack. His eyes jumped all over the hospital room, not meeting Jack's gaze. "You won't want me to come home," he breathed out, slowly.

"Why? Corey. I already know you were with someone. Some dick who hurt you." He tried to keep the anger out of his voice, but Corey flinched anyway.

"I didn't want to. I just needed...I needed..."

"I know. It's okay. I don't blame you, baby. This is all my fault. I shouldn't have ever pushed you so hard."

Corey let a shy smile cross his face. "I did like the party. Before, you know? Where you led me around. I even enjoyed the spanking, but, uh, after." He shook his head a little, closing his eyes, thick wet lashes fluttering against his cheeks. "Not so much."

"I know. I let you down. I shouldn't have left you there."

Corey shrugged. "I shouldn't have gone off with Eric." His voice was barely audible.

"Is that who did this?"

Corey nodded.

"You know his last name? Where he lives?"

"No. I have his phone number."

Jack rubbed his shoulder. "I gave your phone to the detective."

"Okay."

"Corey. You're everything to me." He took Corey's hand and slid their fingers together. "I want you home. I don't care about what you did while you were gone. I just want you home. Safe. I love you."

Corey brought their hands up to his face and kissed the

back of Jack's hand. "I love you, too. I'm so sorry."

"Say you'll come home."

"I'll come home."

Jack leaned over the railing and found Corey's lips. He had to have his mouth. Corey leaned up, letting him take it.

20 Absorption

The doctor came in and ordered another round of blood tests. Corey swore they drew a few gallons out of his veins, but it hadn't really been much. If everything came back clean, they'd let him go home in the morning. He'd asked for them to lower his pain meds. He had a high tolerance for pain, and didn't want to feel so loopy, especially when he knew the detective was coming to talk to him soon.

Dirk had visited him for a little while. He'd been very concerned. Corey felt bad that he'd been dragged into the mess. Dirk was nice, a good friend, but he'd never understand Corey's warped life.

Corey couldn't sleep. His mind was wandering and he lay there watching Jack slide down in a chair. His head hung over the back and his long legs stretched out over the floor. Corey had never wanted the man more.

He wanted to go home and lay next to Jack in that big king sized bed. He wanted to be bent over his knee. He wanted to feel his hard cock inside him. Tears stung his eyes. He'd almost ruined all of this. Jack was being so nice about it, but when Corey closed his eyes, he saw Eric's lean face, blond hair, and that sneer that said he thought Corey was garbage. He wanted to puke at the thought. How could he have been so stupid? He'd convinced himself that he just needed a little pain to keep his emotions under control, but he really needed Jack.

He needed Jack to be his Dom and his lover, to take care of him in every way that he needed. Jack would understand that better than anyone. Why had he spent so much time running from that?

Jack started shuffling around uncomfortably in the chair. "Jack?" Corey called.

His deep blue eyes opened and looked at Corey intently from across the room. "You okay?"

"No. I need you."

In a flash Jack was at his side crooning in his ear softly. "What is it baby? Do you need more pain meds?" Jack took his hand and kissed Corey's head.

"Baby, kick off your shoes and crawl up here with me."

Jack stood back. "Corey, I can't."

"I need you. I need to feel you. And I need you to sleep." Corey pouted, his bottom lip poking out.

Jack sighed and kicked off his shoes. Corey turned over so that the injured side was up, and when Jack slid in beside him, he draped his body over Jack's chest. Jack snuggled him in. "This is better, right?" Corey asked.

"Of course, baby." Jack kissed him on his head again, and closed his eyes. Corey snuggled in and let his mind drift.

Sometime later Corey woke when the nurse shoved another pillow under his head. "Is this okay?" he asked, softly.

"Yeah. As long as you're comfortable. Pain?" It was the nurse Corey liked best. She wore scrubs covered with cute puppy dogs all over them.

"No. I'm good." Corey couldn't hold back his smile as he snuggled down. Jack's soft snoring flowed into the room like music.

The nurse came close to the bed. "I'm glad he's getting some sleep."

"Mm. Me too."

"You know, he hasn't left you for a second. He hasn't been farther than the waiting room. Even when you're other friends left. He wouldn't go. That means something to me, Corey. How 'bout you?"

Corey hadn't known that. It did mean something; it meant everything. "He loves me," Corey whispered, gazing into Jack's face. Jack had said it, but until that moment Corey didn't really believe him.

Corey woke up when Jack slid out of the bed. "Jack?" He felt clingy, wanting to touch his Dom and be held and reassured that Jack wasn't going to leave him or push him away.

"Sh. S'okay, baby. The detective is coming to talk to you. You need to wake up a little, hm?"

Corey nodded and let himself relax. He hated laying on his back. It made things uncomfortable without the meds. He'd slept much better lying across Jack's body. By the smile on Jack's face, Corey thought he'd slept better, too.

Jack wet a towel and wiped Corey's face and neck, gently. His jaw was tight the entire time.

"Are you mad at me?" It was all he could do to hold back tears. If Jack were mad, he thought he'd lose his shit and Jack seemed mad.

"No, baby, but seeing the bruises on you like this makes me want to kill the bastard."

Corey lowered his eyes. "I'm a wreck."

"It's okay. You're allowed to be." He kissed the top of Corey's head. "I'll be out in the waiting room. I won't—"

"No. Please stay." Corey grabbed his hand, squeezing it tight.

Jack leaned against the bed and pushed Corey's bangs to the side. "I thought you'd be more comfortable without me in here. I know. I know it's difficult for you." He swallowed hard around his words.

Corey couldn't face talking about this without support. "I need you here." His voice was barely even a whisper, but Jack heard him.

"He's going to ask about everything. About what you did with this guy."

"He's not going to understand."

Jack pet Corey's hair. "Probably not. But, you need to remember something."

"What?"

"Just because you like a little pain. Just because you like things others don't understand..." Jack shook his head.

"Like being tied up and spanked?"

"Yes. Like that. It doesn't mean you wanted him to knock you around and stab you. He tried to kill you."

"I don't think so. I think he thought he could do whatever he wanted with me. I let him tie my hands. Let him flog me. Let him fuck me. He thought I was. Not worth." Corey's tears poured from his eyes. He couldn't stop them if he'd wanted to.

"That's not true, though. He had no right. Did you talk about your limits first, Corey."

Corey wiped at his tears with the back of his hand. "Yeah. I said no pictures and use a condom. He did."

"Okay. Did you tell him your safe words? Tell him if you said red he had to stop."

"I said it, Jack. I said red but he didn't stop. He got mad." Corey sobbed and Jack's arms were around him, holding him, rubbing his shoulder.

"You're a good boy, Corey. He was wrong and he's going to pay for it. Okay?"

A knock on the door drew Corey's attention. He wiped at his face, clearing the tears. The man that walked in didn't look like much. His broad shoulders filled out his leather jacket, and his slacks showed a thin waist. He was in his thirties, but the lines around his eyes made him look much older. Corey realized he had a hard job, probably saw way worse than Corey's drama. His heart slowed with the thought. "Hello," Corey said.

"I'm Detective Bishop. I'm working your case. How're you feeling?"

Corey shrugged. "Better, but still shitty."

"Yeah, it'll take a while to heal up." Bishop looked up at Jack. "This would probably be better if I talked to Corey by himself a bit."

"No," Corey protested. "I...I'll tell you everything. Answer all your questions, but I need Jack here."

"I'm going to ask about Jack," he said, as if to give Corey a chance to change his mind.

"Okay."

The detective sat on the chair beside the bed, where Jack had tried in vain to sleep. He pulled a pad and pencil out of his back pocket and eased back in the chair. "So, let's start with the basics. What happened, Mr. Roman?"

"Sure. Call me Corey. So I called Eric and he picked me up in front of the club."

"What club?"

"Dragon. Know where that is?"

Jack made a noise behind him. Jack knew which club he meant. "Dragon? Is that where you met this guy?"

Bishop spoke up. "Think I'm asking the questions right now, Mr. Wolfe."

"Sorry." Jack's hand tightened on Corey's shoulder, and Corey knew he was feeling possessive. He knew his Dom. The Dragon club pushed his buttons, but it couldn't be helped now.

"Yeah. I met him there, but I didn't go in then. When he picked me up, it wasn't even open yet."

"What time was it?" Bishop asked, looking in his notebook.

Corey sighed a little and gripped Jack's hand tighter. "It was probably about three or four in the afternoon, maybe a little later. I'm not sure."

Bishop looked up from his pad. "Why aren't you sure?"

"I wasn't thinking about the time. I was upset. I only thought, uh, I just wasn't really thinking clearly."

"What next?" Bishop's soft brown eyes were encouraging. Corey relaxed for the moment, knowing it would get worse.

"He took me to a hotel. I can't even tell you which one."

"I know which one. Go on."

Corey was surprised at his statement, he looked up at Jack. He nodded for Corey to go on. "So, we fooled around, had sex. Then, he attacked me when I was vulnerable."

"What does that mean?"

"S'okay, Corey," Jack said, reassuringly.

"He flogged me until I was floating. I was floating. God, he could have killed me." He hid his face in his hands.

"What does floating mean? Were you on drugs?"

Jack chuckled. "No, it means he was in what some people call subspace. Heard of that? It means he was disconnected. His head wasn't there. It's a very pleasurable state, it's one of the reasons they do it."

"They?" Bishop looked confused.

Corey bit his lip, wanting to let Jack explain, and he did. "Subs. Submissives. The BDSM culture."

Bishops eyes widened, and then he looked like something snapped in place. "Okay. So, he beat you into this, what? This altered state? And then attacked you? Stabbed you?"

Corey nodded.

"What'd you do?"

"I freaked out. I told him to stop. I used my safe word." Jack kissed him on the top of the head. He knew Jack was proud of him for that at least. "That pissed him off, I guess. He choked me. Hit me." Corey took a deep breath. "I ran out of the room. I don't remember anything after that until I woke up here."

Bishop jotted down some notes, then flipped back a few pages. The crinkles between his eyebrows dipped down. "So, you were staying with Dirk because you left Jack. Is that right?"

"Yeah."

"Why?"

"Why what?"

"Why did you leave Jack?"

Corey shook his head. He didn't want to talk about any of this anymore. "It doesn't matter. It doesn't have anything to do with this. I made a mistake going with Eric. He attacked me.

End of story."

"I'm sorry, Mr. Roman. I see how uncomfortable this is, but I have a responsibility to get the whole picture and to make sure that you're safe."

Corey muttered under his breath, but he knew neither Jack nor the detective would hear it.

"What? What are you saying?" Bishop asked, his arms waving in the air.

Corey took a deep breath. "I said that's Jack's job. It's his job to make sure I'm safe. He didn't. I left him."

"Are you back together? Is it his job again?"

Corey nodded, but he was still a little unsure of where he stood with Jack.

Bishop exhaled loudly and flipped through his pad again. "Okay. I think I got this. I just need another minute, but I'd really like to speak with you alone, Mr. Roman. This is important."

Jack bent over and kissed Corey on the mouth and looked him right in the eyes. "It's okay baby. Detective Bishop is doing his job. He's being thorough. You tell him. Whatever he asks. Just tell him the truth. I'll be out in the hall."

Corey let Jack's hand go and watched him move across the room.

Jack stopped and looked at the detective. For a moment, Corey was afraid that there would be more of a confrontation, but Jack surprised him. He reached in his wallet and pulled out a card. "You can call Kenneth Moore if you want more information on the lifestyle or as a character reference." Corey breathed easier for that second that the detective took the card and shook Jack's hand.

But, then Jack left the room, the door swinging shut behind him and Corey's heart pounded like a sledgehammer against his chest. His foundation was gone, and he felt a little like free falling.

"What is it you need to ask, detective?" he asked, staring at the door. The sooner his questions were answered, the sooner Jack could come back into the room.

"I see how you're holding on to him so tight. The way you watched him leave. Are you afraid of him? Really? Your friends will help you. You don't have to go back to him."

Corey's head slowly swiveled to face the detective. "Sir, with all due respect, you don't know what the fuck you're talking about."

"Enlighten me?"

"He's my boyfriend, my Dom, my lover, my protector. If I'd called him instead of getting my fix from a stranger, this wouldn't have happened."

"He assaulted, uh..." Bishop flipped through his pad. "Colin Hayward. Mr. Wolfe said it was about you."

"Yes, it was. Jack, uh, he..."

"I'm not judging you or Mr. Wolfe. I just need to make sure you're okay and make sure I understand this. I feel like I'm missing pieces of this story." He held his hands out, gesturing for more.

Corey closed his eyes. "Jack had a party. To show me off. He spanked me in front of everyone and then left me in the living room. This Hayward guy had something with Jack before and thought it'd be okay to touch me. It wasn't. I was still floating and—"

"That subspace thing?"

"Yes. My head wasn't there, and Hayward. Uh, he assaulted me. Jack went nuts. I lost my shit, totally. I ran. I kept running. I met Eric and thought he could give me a little of what I needed." Corey chuckled at the look on Bishop's face. "I'm a masochist. I need. The pain gets me off. I need to get that fix somewhere safe. Jack is safe, Eric was not. It took me learning the hard way to figure that out."

"This is a lot to take in." Bishop shook his head and stared at his pad.

Corey shrugged. "Listen. I like a little pain. I like to be tied up, flogged, whatever. Jack said that didn't give Eric the right to stab me, to ignore my safe word, to..." Corey had enough, tears were threatening again. "I'm really tired, sir."

"Yeah. Okay. We did our homework, Mr. Roman. We

know who Eric is. I'm assuming that he's stored in your phone under 'XXX' right?"

Corey nodded.

"That's all I need. We're going to arrest him. You may have to say some of this stuff in front of a jury if he doesn't plead out. We'll keep you posted."

"Thank you."

The detective left. Corey felt drained. He stared at the door until Jack finally came back in the room.

21 Recovery

Jack spent nearly thirty minutes of his time with Jillian's friend talking about his upcoming project. He didn't really care if he won the award or what the public thought about it. He didn't even care about the project. After the first half hour, he transferred her over to Dwayne. He was the project manager for this one anyway.

Jillian was Kenneth's sub, but beyond that she had helped Corey out. Repaying the favor was a given, but his heart just wasn't in it.

Once he had Dwayne settled with the interviewer, his deep need to check on Corey had him calling Mick for a ride back to the penthouse. He'd barely let Corey out of his sight since he'd left the hospital. He'd only gone in to work for the interview, and only at Corey's insistence because Jillian had helped him.

Back at home, Corey was snuggled under the covers in the big king size bed in the master bedroom. Jack stripped down to his briefs and climbed in beside him, pulling Corey up to his chest. Corey moaned appreciatively.

"I'm home baby."

Corey's soft, sleepy voice asked, "How'd it go?" Jack loved how cute he was when he first woke up. He never wanted to spend another night without Corey in his arms.

"Fine, fine. How you feeling?"

"Still sleepy."

Jack flipped Corey over on his back and peered down at his face. The bruises around his eye were yellowing and looked much worse than they probably were at that point. There were purple, yellow and green smudges down his neck. The sight made Jack want to kill the fucker that dared mark his boy.

He kissed under Corey's jaw, licking and delicately nibbling until Corey moaned. "I've missed you so much," Jack whispered, trailing his tongue along Cory's collarbone and the hollow of his throat. He couldn't keep his hands from trailing down Corey's chest and caressing every bit of skin he could touch.

"Nice," Corey hissed softly.

Jack continued to kiss his way down, wanting to bring him pleasure. After being gone for so long, he needed to have his hands against Corey's soft skin and his lips eating up his body heat.

He nuzzled up against Corey's cock, and was immediately rewarded with a whimper from Corey. "Mine," Jack moaned, taking him fully into his mouth.

"Jack."

"Shh, baby. I want you to come for me." He dipped down over Corey's cock again, and fluttered his fingertips across his scrotum. "I got you, baby." Jack moaned, letting his lips vibrate across Corey's shaft. A few deep thrusts, and Corey was coming hard down the back of Jack's throat.

Afterward, Jack held Corey close, smiling uncontrollably. He was never going to let Corey go again. He promised himself that he would stuff his ego down and keep his sub safe.

A knock on the front door made Jack jump and Corey shifted in his arms. He wanted to snuggle back down in the warmth, but whoever was at the door pounded again. He got up and pulled on a pair of athletic shorts and headed down the hallway.

He opened the door to see Detective Bishop leaning on the door jam. "Looking for Mr. Roman. His friends said try here?" The last was an awkward question and a demand wrapped up together with a pinch of his thick eyebrows. Bishop wasn't an unattractive man, but he had perpetual bags under his eyes and crow's feet making him appear run down. His rumpled clothes didn't help the image at all.

"Yes. Come in." Jack held his arm up in invitation and followed the detective into the house.

The man stood in his living room, looking around expectantly. "Mr. Roman?"

"I'll get him." Jack walked back to the room and gently shook Corey's shoulder. "Baby," he whispered. "Detective Bishop is here. Time to get up."

Corey rolled over and opened his eyes like two glittery emeralds staring up at him. "Hey?" he asked with a sleep-scratchy voice.

"Sleepy boy, get up. The detective is here."

"Okay." Corey got up and put on shorts and an oversized t-shirt. Jack thought he looked very sexy, and wanted nothing more than to get him back into bed. To hell with the detective, but he bit back his reactions. He needed to give Corey comfort, not put him on edge.

He wrapped his arms around Corey and kissed the top of his head, nuzzling into his dark curls. "You okay?"

"Yeah." Corey turned his face up, silently asking for more kisses, and Jack was quick to oblige him, smothering Corey's mouth with his own.

"Come on." He directed Corey out of the room. Things had been so nice between them since Corey had been released from the hospital. It felt settled. He didn't want the detective stirring things up again; he wanted to move on.

"Mr. Roman," the detective addressed Corey formally.

"Please, call me Corey." He offered his hand to the detective to shake.

After a brief shake, Bishop cleared his throat. "So, he made a deal with the D.A. and it's over. He got probation and time served."

Jack interrupted, "So, he's out? Out of jail?"

Bishop nodded. "Yes. Since he didn't get out on bail before. Released him this morning. I wanted to make sure you knew."

"That's fine," Corey said. His voice was calm. "I appreciate you coming over."

Jack was concerned that Corey wasn't processing everything. He didn't seem upset at all. "Corey?" he started to ask.

"It's fine, Jack. I'll never see him again. He doesn't know me or you. I changed my phone number. He never picked me up at the house. So, I'm not worried. Even if I did see him, I wouldn't ever go off with him again. I'm not afraid."

The detective gave a curt nod, his eyes on Corey's face. "If you do ever need anything, or, uh, anything, you still have my number?" Jack would have been jealous, but he knew the detective was just being protective, doing his job. He knew firsthand how easy it was to slide into protective mode with Corey. He seemed so vulnerable and sweet most of the time. Jack wanted to spend the rest of his life protecting him.

He shook the detective's hand and thanked him, simultaneously dismissing him. No need to push it.

When Jack came back in the living room, he couldn't help notice the disgusted look on Corey's face. His nose was crinkled up, and his pallor went green. He sat on the couch seeming to study the rest of the room.

"You okay?"

"No." Corey shook his head. "Honestly, Jack. I hate it here. I hate this place. I'm sorry." Tears pooled up in his eyes. "Too many...too much...It's just cold and it's yours and..." He cleared his throat. "I'm sorry. It's just that Detective Bishop got me thinking about everything again." Corey's reaction was understandable. He blew out a long breath. "God Jack, I need the pain—yes. Definitely, but I need your love too. I have to feel important to you, Jack. I have to...to feel wanted for me and not just for my submission."

There was still a nasty spot on the carpet, faded to a pink instead of the blood red that it had been. Jack watched Corey's eyes land on it, then look away. The memories were intense. They needed a chance to start over. Corey was right. He deserve to be comfortable, to feel at home, to be loved.

"It's okay. We can move, baby. It's just a place." Home to Jack meant Corey in his arms, safe, not the stupid penthouse. "Whatever you need, baby."

Love and sex and BDSM warped together in Jack's head. He knew he had to separate those things more. "I don't think I learned this right."

"What do you mean?" Corey gave him a beseeching look. Jack really wanted to fix this. He sighed when Corey reached out to touch Jack's hand and pull him down beside him, but Jack pulled away.

He needed to talk about all of this, so Corey could have everything he needed. "I...I don't think I really know how to be a good Dom or a good boyfriend. I love you. I know that much. More than anything, Corey, I love you."

"I love you, too," he whispered.

Jack knelt in front of him, staring into his eyes, into his soul, hoping he would understand. "I'm willing to work at it. I want you with me, in my arms. Safe. Happy. We both need to be happy, but especially you, Corey. Because that's how I know things are working. When you're happy." For a moment, neither said anything, but Jack needed to move forward. "What do we do?" He was supposed to be the Dom, to make the decisions, but he couldn't do that if he didn't know where Corey's head was.

"I need." He wrapped his arms around himself. "I need to trust you again, Jack," he murmured. Jack hated his lack of confidence. Guilt coursed through him, knowing he'd done that. It wasn't what he'd ever wanted.

"I know." He rubbed his hands on the leather sofa on either side of Corey's legs. "I...I'm dealing with things. Kenneth has been helping me work through it. I meant what I said in the hospital, Corey."

Corey pursed his lips together as if physically trapping the words inside his mouth.

"Say whatever you want, Corey. I won't leave or get mad. We need to work through this."

He huffed. "You're such an asshole sometimes. You treat me like a thing, not a person. I need you to see me." Corey touched his own chest. "Not what I'm wearing or eating or what job I have. And not just what we do in the bedroom."

Jack stood up and ran his hand through his thick hair. Thinking about these things was not easy. Talking about it was even worse. He put his hands on his hips and took a long deep breath like Kenneth had started making him do. Then he turned to face Corey. He was so worth whatever mental vomit Jack had to do.

"I've never really talked about this with you or anyone."

"Jack?" Corey asked, compassion coloring his name on Corey's lips.

"I have to have complete control. That part we've talked about. I said that way back then, when we first got together. Remember?"

"Yes," Corey answered, biting at his bottom lip and making Jack want desperately to skip this conversation and just take him to bed.

"Corey. It's not because I'm an asshole. Okay, not *just* that I'm an asshole." Jack waved his hand in the air. "I know, I know. I'm certainly an asshole. It's just that it's more than that. Okay?"

Corey didn't say anything, just looked at him with wonder and silent pleading.

Jack wasn't sure how to even start. "So, my parents. They kind of sucked."

"So? My parents suck. Don't know too many that don't. At least for gay boys."

"True, but mine took it to a whole new level. I mean they, uh, they..." Jack paced across the floor.

"Jack, come on. Just tell me." He didn't say it like he was running out of patience, but rather that he knew Jack needed to say it.

"My parents liked to party. There was always something going on. I don't remember much of it because I was young. They were, well they seemed, you know? Self-absorbed. And I'd be okay with that but they had a kid." Jack touched his chest. "I wasn't enough."

"I know how that feels."

"Oh, baby! I know you do." In a flash Jack crossed the room and pulled Corey up into a deep hug. "You don't have to let them do that to you anymore. If you don't want anything to do with them, just don't call them or go see them, unless you want to. You're more than enough for me and that matters so much more."

"I don't know how I feel about them right now, but it's nothing for us to worry about or deal with. At least right now."

Jack pulled back and gazed into Corey's precious eyes. "I promise. I'm here for you. I meant what I said. You mean everything to me. No matter what. It's important to me that you're happy. Nothing else matters."

Corey cupped Jack's face. "That's not true. You need to be happy too."

"I'm happy when you are."

Corey chuckled and Jack loved the sound. "Jack. You're so sappy. So, what about your parents? You never talk to me about them."

"I don't even let myself think about them most of the time."

"Why?"

"They're dead. They killed themselves."

"What?"

"They left me. I wasn't even ten years old." Jack leaned back on the couch, shoulders dropping, and letting all of his crap fall from his chest.

"Jack? What happened?"

"They went to some stupid party. I think it was a swinger party or fetish. I'm not sure because at the time nobody wanted to tell me what happened. It took a long time to find out.

Eventually, I dragged it out of my aunt. My mom's sister. She was my only other family."

"And?" Corey grabbed Jack's thigh, offering comfort.

Jack hated to admit how much he needed that comfort in order to continue. "So, they were doing, uh, breath play. She died. My dad accidentally killed her. Then, he put a bullet through his head and left me there. Defenseless."

Corey looked up at him with concern and love in his eyes, where Jack had been expecting pity. "Jack. You never—"

"Like I said. I don't even think about it anymore, babe."

"So, your aunt took you in?"

"No."

"What do you mean? Didn't you just say she was your only family?"

"Yeah, but she didn't want me. I can't blame her much. She was an old biddy. She was single and traveled and I guess having a ten year old hanging around would have seriously cramped her style."

"What did you do?"

"Foster care. From one place to another. Over and over. Always the new kid and I was scrawny. I got picked on and bullied. Fuck! I can't do this." Jack buried his face in the palms of his hands. He'd had enough, the exposure leaving him raw.

Corey wrapped his arms around Jack, then climbed in his lap. "You're not scrawny now, Jack."

Jack wiped a rebellious tear from under his eye.

"I love you, Jack. No matter what."

Jack pulled Corey up in his arms, holding him tight, kissing the top of his head. "Oh God, Corey."

"I'm here," Corey said, rubbing his hands along Jack's arms. "I'm here."

Jack started crying in earnest then, burying his head in Corey's chest. "Oh, God! Ah!"

"Shh, I've got you."

They rocked back and forth, arms around each other. It could have been five minutes or five hours. It didn't matter. Jack could have stayed wrapped up in Corey forever, just like that with his face against Corey's shoulder. "After I finally drug the whole story out of my aunt, I decided that I needed to be in control of my own life and everything in it. So, when I graduated high school, I didn't look back."

"The rest is history?"

"No. Not really. There's more in there, but that's all I can deal with tonight. The worst of it."

"Jack, baby?"

"Yes?"

"Let's, uh, go in the bedroom and you can boss me around? Okay?"

"Damn that sounds good, baby."

22 Domination

Jack fiddled with his laptop before setting it on the coffee table. He wanted to throw it across the room. Their search for a new home was going ridiculously slow. He was the *God-Damned New Cabell Real Estate King* for Christ's sakes!

Corey walked in and set a snifter of brandy beside the laptop, then sat on the floor beside the table, in a ready submissive pose. He wore a pair of tight white boxer shorts and nothing else, as he knelt with his hands behind his back and his head bent. Waiting.

Jack's cock pulsed and plumped at the site. He wanted to dig his fingers through Corey's dark curls and kiss his neck and his lips. They'd been doing a lot more kissing and relatively vanilla sex, for them, since he'd been released from the hospital, and Jack knew they'd both be wanting more soon. Corey seemed to be more ready than Jack.

"I think we need some ice-cream, sir," Corey said softly, not raising his head, but Jack could see how he trembled, just that little bit.

"What do you want, Corey? How far are you ready to go?"

"I need..."

"Corey. You've only been out of the hospital a few weeks and your health and safety is my first concern."

Corey raised his head, eyes sparkling. "I know. But, I need this. I need something. Pain."

"I don't know if you're ready," Jack lied. Obviously, Corey was ready. He was begging for it. Jack knew deep in his heart that *he* wasn't ready. He didn't want to hurt Corey in any way. Now that he was back, he wanted to cherish him and love him and smother him with kisses. He took a deep breath. Corey needed more than his affection. "I don't want to hurt you. I don't want to see you hurt. After what happened. I can't even. Corey."

Sinking back on his heels, Corey stared at Jack with a grim determination that he hadn't seen before. "Jack. I'm not playing. I need this. You're my Dom. If you can't do this, I'm going to have to find someone that will. I need to trust you. Trust you to take care of me. In every way."

Jack knew he had to suck it up. This wasn't about him. It never had been. Corey was his world and he'd do whatever he could to make him feel good. "Kenneth said Jillian was going to talk to you about a therapist."

"Yes, sir. I made an appointment, but I don't have health insurance."

"I'll take care of it."

"Jack, it's not going to change my need for pain."

"It doesn't have to." Jack stood up and offered his hand to Corey, pulling him up off the floor and directing him to the bedroom. "Okay, baby. We'll play. But don't expect the single tail or anything like that."

"Whatever you say, Sir."

"Make sure you use your safe words, Corey. If something doesn't feel right, you need to say. I don't want to hurt your injury or anything."

"I promise, Jack."

Jack nudged Corey with his hip. "What?"

"Sir. I promise, sir."

"Okay."

When he had Corey standing in front of the bed, Jack reached out to his waist and pulled his underwear down, dropping them to the floor. Corey looked up at him with pleading eyes, making his stomach flutter. "Hold your arms out," he commanded before turning to his toy chest.

He found his favorite leather cuffs and worked them around Corey's wrists. He clamped a short chain between them, giving Corey little room to move around.

"Lay across the bed on your stomach. Arms over your head. Don't move."

Jack grabbed a short paddle and dropped his pants and shirt to the floor before climbing up in the bed next to his sub. "I'm going to work you over a little. Okay?"

"Yes, sir." Corey's reply was breathy and he wiggled his ass.

"Be still." He placed his hand at the small of Corey's back over the little white scars left over from the single tail. He still struggled with whether or not he liked the permanent markings but Corey didn't seem to mind them, so for the moment he'd leave off.

He used the flat side of the paddle and warmed Corey's ass up nicely. "You okay, Corey?"

"Mmm..."

Jack smiled. He could tell even that little bit already had Corey floating. "Good," he whispered and started prepping Corey's ass. They'd been going at it a lot, making love almost daily, so he needed very little prep. They were back to using condoms until Corey passed his next lab work, though, so Jack rolled the rubber over his hard cock.

He grabbed Corey's hips, pulling him up off the bed. "I'm going to fuck you now, Corey."

He received another, "Mmm..." and took that as a good sign.

He pushed in hard, not giving Corey a moment to catch his breath or get used to the feel. He knew Corey would love it. He snapped his hips, hard and fast, fucking Corey like he knew his sub wanted. When Corey started moaning, close to the edge, Jack growled out, "Don't you dare come, Corey. Not until I say."

"Yes," he moaned.

Jack leaned over and bit Corey's shoulder, hard enough to

make Corey shudder beneath him. The movement sent Jack over the edge and he came hard, filling up the detestable condom. When he was finished, he pulled out. "Roll over Corey," he demanded, as he cleaned up, dropping the condom in the wastebasket.

Corey's cock was hard and purple and twitching as if begging Jack for release. He almost snickered, but then saw the pained expression on Corey's face. "It's okay, Corey. You know I have you, baby."

"Yes, Jack, sir."

Jack went back to his toy box and pulled out a pair of nipple clamps. They'd help. After fastening them to Corey's nipples and watching eagerly as Corey moaned and gyrated on the bed, he went back to his toy chest. He needed something else. Corey was riding the edge, but he wanted to give his lover something to remember, but not too extreme.

After a few minutes, he saw the white paraffin candles and grabbed one. This was just going to be a little enhancement, not a huge hot wax scene. Jack had to go to the kitchen to get a match and a big tumbler of ice water, just in case. When he got back to the room, Corey hadn't moved. He lay on his back, legs spread, hands bound over his head. He breathed hard through is nose. "Close your eyes, Corey."

He did—without missing a beat. Jack walked slowly up to the bed. The candle was already starting to drip down the side, so he tipped it onto Corey's stomach, not even an inch away from his cock. Corey gasped and jerked.

"Hold still, baby."

A strangled noise came from Corey's throat as he forced himself to relax. "That's it, baby. You're doing so good," Jack purred to him, as he dripped the candle wax on his chest between his nipples, eliciting another moan. "So sexy, baby." Jack gave each of his thighs a couple of drops, successively. Corey gasped, but held still.

"Oh God, Jack. Drip it on my cock. God, please."

Jack wanted to deny him, afraid of hurting him when he hadn't experimented enough with this type of play. The white wax dripping along his chest and stomach was pretty hot, though. Corey had a high tolerance for pain, but that made it even more dangerous. Jack could hurt him before he even noticed.

"Okay. Give me a second." Jack went to the bathroom and wet a washcloth. When he came back, Corey was writhing in the bed, his body begging for more with its motion.

"Corey. If this feels too hot at all. You tell me. I don't want any damage to your cock. Got it."

"Yes, sir. Please."

"Okay. Keep your eyes closed."

He held the candle much higher above Corey than with the other body parts, giving the wax time to cool on the way down, but it also caused the wax to splatter more. Dots of white splashed over his cock, balls and hips.

Corey gasped. "Oh, God, Jack!"

Jack blew out the candle and tossed it on the dresser, then grabbed Corey's cock with the wet wash cloth. Corey sighed and his shoulders relaxed into the mattress, as his cock exploded. He didn't even have to stroke him.

"That's a good boy!"

"Thank you, sir."

Jack smiled. He'd made Corey happy. *I can do this!* Jack shouldn't have ever doubted his ability to take care of his sub in the first place. If he would have just stayed centered around Corey, they wouldn't have had so much difficulty with this. Jack needed to remember that.

"I love you, Corey," he said, but Corey was already asleep. Jack gently removed his cuffs, letting him curl up on his side. They could get rid of the wax mess later.

23 Domestication

Six months later

Corey unlocked the front door, letting himself in. Every time he came through the front door and stood in the large foyer, he couldn't believe how happy he was.

Jack had sold his penthouse and bought this lovely place for Corey. It was warm, devoid of white leather; that had stayed with the penthouse. No, this place was brown and cream and warm. It had a huge fireplace in the living room and plush creamy carpet. The huge master suite had a giant walk-in closet and a king sized bed that Corey shared completely with Jack. There was a second room that they both used for office space, and most importantly, there was a third room that they'd set up just for playing. It had hard wood floors, taupe walls, a bondage horse, spanking bench, and a large cabinet. Jack was talking about trading out the horse for a swing. Corey didn't care, as long as he got strapped in.

They'd picked out everything together, and aside from clothing and personal items, the only thing they brought from the penthouse was the *Zang* that Corey liked so much. They hung it in the dining room. Corey liked the way the colors looked in the last light of the day streaming in through the window. He liked how Jack had made him the center of their world, even more.

Corey loved the entire house. He loved his relationship

with Jack. He loved his new job that Jillian had helped him land. He loved studying for his C.P.A. and he was even letting Jack pay for it.

"Jack!" he called out. "I'm home."

Jack walked down the hallway. He wore his black and red leather shorts and he had his hands behind his back. "You're late."

Corey let a smile quirk up his lip. He knew he wasn't late. His Dom was making up something to punish him for. "Oh! I must have lost track of time, Sir." He had a hard time keeping a straight face.

"You think it's funny?"

"No, Sir." Corey set his keys and wallet on the sofa table and walked toward Jack.

"Then, take off your clothes for me, Corey."

Corey happily started stripping.

"Don't you know what day it is?" Jack asked, as Corey dropped his pants.

"No?"

"It's our anniversary. I can't believe you forgot."

"I...uh?" He had no idea it was their anniversary. He'd been so busy lately, he couldn't even guess at what day it was. "Jack, I'm sorry."

"It's okay, baby. It's my job to remind you and I didn't. I wanted to surprise you."

"I'm surprised."

Jack brought his hands out from behind his back and stretched them out. He was holding a long thin black box. "I had this made for you."

Corey sank to his knees and took the box. He opened it to see a thick black chain. It was masculine, yet beautiful.

"Here," Jack said, taking the chain and flipping it over. "Look."

The inside was engraved. "Corey and Jack" and the date. Corey felt tears swelling up in his eyes. Jack got on his knees in front of Corey and kissed his eyelids. He put the chain around Corey's neck. "Want to go see how that looks?"

Corey nodded, choking back tears.

"Go look. Then, meet me in the playroom." Jack wiggled his eyebrows, making Corey giggle.

He went into the bathroom and stared at himself in the mirror. His black, curly hair and pale skin looked healthy. The chain was gorgeous and looked expensive. Corey felt proud, honored, and loved.

They'd come such a long, long way. He'd come such a long way. He blew out a shaky breath, thinking about everything that had happened in the past two years. Meeting Jack had sent him over the edge and back again, but he was finally learning to cope with his overly developed need for pain and domination. His new therapist was helping him understand that a lot of his issues were from not properly coping with his fucked up parents. Corey needed to be the center of Jack's world because he'd never been that before; never been the center of his parent's world when he needed it most.

Corey had vowed to ignore his parents as they had ignored him for so many years, and he found with Jack and the larger BDSM community supporting him, it wasn't much of a loss. It still hurt, but he could at least channel that in a healthier way.

He still needed the pain and the submission, but they were controlling it in a more constructive manner. His therapist he'd had as a kid had made him feel bad about his urges. She'd been useless for figuring out how his need for attention had warped with the need for pain and then got all mixed up with his onset of puberty and being gay. She had confused him more than he already was. Most of the time, he just told her what she wanted to hear and moved on.

His new therapist was helping him untangle all of that and helping him understand how his body and brain associated pain with love and caring. She helped him set up new rules with Jack, too.

Jack wasn't allowed to ignore him or leave him in a room alone for any extended amount of time when they were playing. If he left the room, Corey had to know why and when he'd be back. Jack was also allowed a safe word. Instead of abruptly leaving a scene in the middle, if he couldn't handle it or thought it was too much for Corey, he could call yellow or red, just like Corey. The new rules let his heart beat free from any barbed wire constrictions.

They still weren't playing with others. Neither of them could handle that. Kenneth had also helped them find a new group because they couldn't handle seeing Colin either. The new group was supportive and he was making new sub-friends, but Jillian was still his favorite.

Corey shook off the memories, anticipating what was coming next. He took a quick piss, washed his hands, and hurried to the playroom. He liked having anniversaries. He loved having Jack.

When he walked in, Jack was standing in the middle of the room with his favorite leather crop held loosely in his hands. His dark hair had grown out a little and curled around his ears. He hadn't shaved either, the dark scruff trimming his jaw and chin, looking so masculine, and his eyes, so intense, had Corey shaking with desire.

He obediently dropped to his knees in front of Jack and laced his arms together behind his back. His eyes were on Jack's lovely bare feet. Perfectly manicured, long thin toes, they had to be the sexiest feet Corey had ever seen. He never got tired of seeing them, especially when he wore the leather shorts. Jack's legs seemed to go on forever in those shorts.

"Corey. You've been such a good boy. You've been doing everything you're supposed to do. It makes me proud."

"Thank you, sir."

"Are you happy, Corey?" Jack asked. The question wasn't unexpected. Since they'd started playing again, almost every session started or ended with this. It felt comforting.

"Yes. Very happy, sir."

"I want you to be able to tell me what you need. I want you to be happy. You understand that? Corey?"

"Yes, sir. I understand," Corey answered easily.

"Do you like your chain?"

"Yes. Very much, sir. Thank you."

"Good. What's your safe words?"

Corey smiled. He still rarely said either of them. "Red to stop. Yellow to slow down."

"Are you going to use them?"

"Only if I need to, sir."

Jack chuckled. "Okay, Corey. Remember, I can use them too. Now, on the bench."

Corey loved getting spanked. He leaned eagerly over the bench. Jack came up behind him, skimming his hand down Corey's thighs. "I have something else for you," he said. Corey didn't ask what, he knew he would find out at Jack's own pace.

He fiddled with Corey's ankles for a minute and then laughed. Corey loved the sexy, playful laugh he heard when they played. Jack had really loosened up during their sessions. "Close your legs, Corey."

Corey tried to obey, but he was restrained. "What? Jack?"

"Look, Corey."

Corey turned halfway, twisting his torso, only to look down and see that Jack had him strapped into a brand new spreader bar. "Oh, I like that."

"I do, too. Turn around." Jack came behind him and shoved his body a little higher on the bench. "Good?"

"Yes."

"I invited your friends over for drinks tonight. So, we need to hurry."

"What?"

Jack laughed again. "Yes, baby. Dirk, Stan, Jillian, and a few others from the group. Detective Bishop might even be here."

"Wow. Then, you better spank me now."

"Don't go getting pushy, baby."

The first smack came down hard in the center of Corey's ass, making him wiggle and moan.

"Be still, baby," Jack said. "I don't want you falling."

"Yes, sir."

A few more overlapping smacks had Corey completely

relaxed and floating. He knew his ass would be red and Jack would be hard as a rock. He smiled and enjoyed the peaceful sensations streaming through his head, where nothing else mattered. It didn't take long before Jack was shoving his cock into Corey's ass, hard. Corey moaned out with the pleasure. "More, Jack. Please."

"God, I love it when you're like this baby. So wanton and free."

Corey loved it, too.

-The End.

Lynn Michaels

Wanton Playlist
Wolves (You Got Me) by Dreamers
Treat by Kasabian
Toxic by Britney Spears
Tear In My Heart by Twenty One Pilots
Take Me Back by Kongos
Somebody New by Joywave
Sex and Candy by Marcy Playground
Same Damn Life by Seether
Room to Breathe by You Me At Six
The River by Manchester Orchestra
Pet by A Perfect Circle
Panic Switch by Silversun Pickups
Pain by Three Days Grace
Never Gonna Leave This Bed by Maroon 5
My Body by Young The Giant
Miserable by Lit
Little Monster by Royal Blood
Just A Phase by Incubus
An Island by Chevelle
Iron Moon by Chelsea Wolfe
I've Got Friends by Manchester Orchestra
I'm The Only One by Melissa Etheridge
I'm So Sick by Flyleaf
I Am by AWOLNATION
Hurts So Good by John Mellencamp
Happy by Mudvayne
Hands Down by Dashboard Confessional
Get Stoned by Hinder
Control by Puddle of Mud
Cold by Crossfade
Black Hole Sun by Soundgarden
Bad Habit by The Kooks
Animal I Have Become by Three Days Grace
Against The Wall by Steve Perry
Afraid by The Neighborhood
Adrenalize by In This Moment
Addicted To Pain by Alter Bridge

ABOUT THE AUTHOR

Lynn Michaels lives and writes in Tampa, Florida where the sun is hot and the Sangria is cold. Lynn is the newest addition to Rubicon Fiction, and she loves reading and writing about hot men in love.

Visit and LIKE on Facebook at:

https://www.facebook.com/pages/Lynn-Michaels/1450504665203028

http://rubiconwriting.com/lynn-michaels/

Lynn Michaels supports the Trevor project where LBGQ teens can get help http://www.thetrevorproject.org/
If you are any teen you know is feeling suicidal please share this number where trained coucelors are there to help: 866-488-7386.

ALSO BY LYNN MICHAELS

In the world of Supercross, taking the holeshot means one racer leaps ahead of the crowd and into first place, leaving the rest of the pack behind. If Supercross racer Davey McAllister knows anything, it's how to take the holeshot. When the hot rising-star mechanic, Tyler Whitmore, shows up in his bed, Davey does just that.

But, dating a competitor's mechanic threatens to blow his ride if anyone finds out. With the fear of losing his sponsors, he has to keep his love life completely under cover, but Davey is in deep and wants to tell the world how much he loves Tyler.

Tyler Whitmore wants to be out of the closet, but dating the competition is a death sentence for his career. Overprotective of Davey's reputation and his own dreams, Tyler refuses to commit to his lover and is afraid of falling hard. Will they ever be able to find their way through the Premiere racing league pitfalls and acknowledge their love?

Now Available on Amazon or All Romance Ebooks

Lines On The Mirror

Martin has always done everything his parents ever asked, never making waves, but never learning how to say no either. Then his new partying neighbors introduce him to a different lifestyle that pushes his limits.

The only thing keeping him grounded is getting back in touch with his first love, Daltrey, who moved across the country when they were still teenagers. Now, he's a successful artist and plays by his own rules. He wants Martin but won't compromise his morals.

When Martin lets his new friends drag him down until he hits bottom, can he ever find his way back to Daltrey and take control of his life?

Now Available on Amazon or All Romance Ebooks

Made in the USA
Charleston, SC
02 April 2016